ALSO BY MOLLY GILES
Rough Translations

Creek Walk
and other stories

Molly Giles

SCRIBNER PAPERBACK FICTION
Published by Simon & Schuster

SCRIBNER PAPERBACK FICTION
Simon & Schuster Inc.
Rockefeller Center
1230 Avenue of the Americas
New York, NY 10020

First Scribner Paperback Fiction edition 1998
Published by arrangement with Papier-Mache Press and Molly Giles

SCRIBNER PAPERBACK FICTION and design are
trademarks of Simon & Schuster Inc.
Designed by Leslie Austin
Manufactured in the United States of America

1 3 5 7 9 10 8 6 4 2

Library of Congress Cataloging-in-Publication Data
Giles, Molly.
Creek walk and other stories / Molly Giles.
—1st Scribner Paperback Fiction ed.
p.   cm.
1. Women—Social life and customs—Fiction. I. Title.
PS3557.I34465C7   1998
813'.54—dc21   98-29866
CIP

ISBN 0-684-85287-X

Grateful acknowledgment is made to the following publications which first published some of the material in this book:

San Francisco Stories, Vol. 1, No. 2, 1980 for "The Language Burier"; *New England Review*, Vol. 3, No. 2, Winter 1980 for "Leaving the Colonel"; *Five Fingers Review*, No. 2, 1984 for "Talking to Strangers"; *Zyzzyva*, Vol. II, No. 2, Summer 1986 for "Cruise Control"; *Writing on the Edge*, Vol. I, No. 2, Spring 1990 and *San Francisco Focus*, December 1993 for "Untitled"; *Crosscurrents*, Vol. 9, No. 1, 1990 and *McCall's*, Vol. CXVIII, No. 2, November 1990 for "Maximum Security"; *The Greensboro Review*, No. 49, Winter 1990–91 for "The Same Old Story"; *Shenandoah*, Vol. 41, No. 2, 1991, *Pushcart Prize XVII* (Pushcart Press, 1992), and *Love Stories for the Rest of Us* (Simon & Schuster, 1994) for "War"; *Sideshow 93* (Somersault Press, 1992), *Pushcart Prize XVIII* (Pushcart Press, 1993), and *Sudden Fiction* (Norton, 1996) for "The Writers' Model"; *Faultline*, Vol. 1, Spring 1993 and *Sideshow 94* (Somersault Press, 1993) for "Smoke and Mirrors"; *Love's Shadow* (The Crossing Press, 1993) and *More* (New Zealand: February 1994) for "Survival in the Wilderness"; *Writers' Harvest* (Harcourt Brace, 1994) for "Beginning Lessons"; *The Tampa Review*, No. 8, Spring 1994 for "The Blessed Among Us"; *The Marin Arts Review*, 1988 for "Creek Walk"; and *Witness*, Vol. IX, No. I, 1995 for "Can You Ever Forgive Me."

to my daughters,
Gretchen, Rachel, and Devon

These stories were read and critiqued in early drafts by many fine fellow writers, and I would like to thank all the wonderful drop-in, drop-out, and regular members of my writing group, which at various times included Paul Bendix, Jane Ciabattari, Lucy Ferriss, Susan Harper, Betty Hodson, Francis Mayes, Sara McAulay, Amelia Mosley, Lorraine Sintetos, and Jane Vandenburgh. Thanks too to Audrey Ferber, Amy Tan, and Jean Thompson, who supported this collection and helped me shuffle the stories into order. And last, warm thanks to Gina Berriault, Cap Lavin, Jim Leigh, and Leo Litwak. They were my teachers, and I am still learning from them.

Contents

War

THE FIRST THINGS I NOTICED when I got back were all the dead plants in the yard. It was as if he'd played God with the garden hose, because the bush beans and peas were all right, but the tomatoes and peppers and corn had dried out. I always like to follow his reasoning when I can, and this, I figured, was his passive-aggressive way of killing what he considered Latin vegetables as a way of punishing me for going to Nicaragua. If I'd gone to Belfast he'd have killed the potatoes, if I'd gone to Lebanon he'd have killed the eggplant. You have to know him to understand how his mind works, and then you have to explain it to him because he pretends not to know himself. I don't bother to do this anymore; since the divorce he's on his own. I just observe.

His truck was gone—only an oil stain to show where he'd parked on the grass the whole time—and he'd put a new latch on the gate that was so complicated I had to set my duffel bag down to figure it out. I'd just about decided I'd have to climb over when Cass came running out the front door and down the path toward me. We gripped hands and tried to kiss through the grids. "Are you all right?" I asked.

"I'm fine," she said. She laughed. "Why wouldn't I be?" She slid the gate open and held her arms up, just like she used to do when she was a baby, but she is nine now, and almost too heavy to lift. "You're the one we've been worried about," she said.

"We?"

"Daddy said you might go to jail down there, and then you'd never get out."

"Your father," I said, "has wish-fulfillment fantasies."

"I'm so glad you're not in jail," Cass murmured, as I hugged her tight and swung her around. "I've missed you so much."

I'd missed her too. It had only been ten days but I felt as if I'd returned from another century. Cass felt huge in my arms, and solid, and astonishingly American, with her pink cheeks and bubblegum smell. She was wearing an old tie-dyed T-shirt of mine and brand new sandals, with, I couldn't help noticing, extremely high heels. He must have enjoyed that; he liked to buy her things he knew I wouldn't approve of. The last time he stayed with her he bought her a white rabbit fur jacket—"real fur," he kept saying, as if the slaughter of helpless animals was an act to be proud of. We'd had such a fight about it Cass had taken the jacket off and thrown it at us both. Cass—we agree on this at least—deserves better parents.

She helped me with my bag and we went into the house, talking all the way. "You were in the paper," she said. "They had a big article on the peace conference and they had your name and everything, and Mrs. Bettinger read it to my class and said you were a heroine."

"A what?" I laughed. I was pleased, but I'd seen too many real heroes and heroines in the last few days. "My main job was to make lists," I told Cass. "It wasn't exciting. I gave a few speeches but mostly I just helped people get off one bus and get onto another." I set my bag down. "How was it for you here? Did you have fun?"

"Not really," Cass said.

I nodded, sympathetic, and glanced across the front room toward the couch. You could tell it had had quite a workout while I'd been gone. There were three big dents in the cushions. The coffee table had been pulled in close, with the remote control at arm's reach, and there were new circle stains on the wood where his ale bottles had been set down, night after night.

"It looks like he slept on that couch," I said.

"He did."

"Every night?" I stepped closer. I could practically see him there, one hand over his mouth as he snored, the other hand over his crotch. "Just like he used to do when we were married," I marveled. "Did he take his clothes off at least?"

"He said there wasn't any point," Cass said. "He'd just have to wear them the next day."

"What about his shoes?"

"I think he took his shoes off."

"And you?"

"Me?" Cass laughed. "You want to know what I slept in?"

"No. I want to know—were you lonely? With him falling asleep in front of TV every night?"

"No," Cass said. "I didn't mind it."

I looked into her face. There were no dark circles under her eyes, no pinch to her lips, no sign of neglect.

"He never talks," I reminded her.

"We had popcorn every night. Kentucky Fried twice. Pizza three times. One night we just had soda and chips."

I shuddered. All those home-cooked casseroles I had left in the freezer— ignored. The vegetarian cookbooks left out on the counter—unread. I pulled off my sweater and looked around. The house felt different but in a way I couldn't define, dirtier somehow, although there were no signs of dirt or disorder. The ferns were all dry in their pots but alive. The books I'd been studying before I left were still on the table, collecting dust and overdue fines, and the Spanish language tapes my lover, Greg, had smuggled off an Army base were still threaded through the cassette deck.

"It's good to be home," I said, not too sure. "But it smells funny. Do you smell anything?"

"Like what?"

"Like socks. Old socks. And...machine parts? And, I don't know, musk?"

"No. It smells like home to me."

"I think I'm going through culture shock," I admitted. "Everything down there smelled like lime trees and sewage. And the people had so little. We have so much more. This room has enough...stuff...to furnish an entire village."

I had a great urge to start carting things out to the sidewalk—lamps we didn't need, extra chairs, the wicker chest, the TV set, the couch—things other people could use. Then I wanted to scrub, and air, and wash all the windows. But I was tired; the flight back had been a long one, and the conference had worn me out. I felt if I closed my eyes for a second I'd see Alejandra or one of the soldiers and they'd be more real to me than this room. "It's a strange phenomenon," I said to Cass in my best speaker's voice, "but the more you know the less you know. You know?"

"I know," Cass giggled.

"Brought you some presents." I crouched by my pack and started to pull out the books. As always, I'd bought too many books—"Who," he used to say, "are you going to pay to read them all for you?" I had a lot of newspapers too; it's endlessly amazing to me, the news we don't get in the States—and my address book was jammed with new names and there were letters I'd promised to forward and articles I'd promised to try and get published. Finally I found the bright embroidered shirt I'd bought Cass and the friendship bracelets the Mendoza children had woven for her. I also brought out the big seashell I'd found on the beach. "You know how I hate to go shopping," I apologized, "and there wasn't much to buy anyway. I almost brought you some bullet shells I found lying in the street, but then I decided to bury them instead. Maybe someone will find them in a thousand years and say, 'Gee, I wonder what humans used to use these for?' "

Cass smiled, the seashell balanced perfectly in her palm. I kissed her and straightened and went into the kitchen to see if he'd remembered to feed the cats or water the basil in the windowsill. The basil was long gone and it looked like he'd dumped coffee grounds or something on the pots. The cats looked healthy enough but they were so glad to see me, butting their old heads against my throat when I picked them up, that I knew he'd kept them locked out the whole time. I pulled burrs from their fur as I went through the mail. There was a nice letter from Señora Ruiz, thanking me for my speech, and a card from the head of the Direct Aid Committee. There was nothing from Greg. Unless he took it, I thought. But why would he take a letter from Greg? He doesn't know who Greg is, and even if he did, he wouldn't care. "One of your little hippie friends," he'd say. "One of your New Left Overs." He would take one look at Greg, who is six years younger than I, and a therapist to boot, then shake his head. "Sonny," he'd say, "if you want to sleep with your mother why don't you just go sleep with your mother?"

I put down the mail and glanced at the message pad on the kitchen wall. There in that stingy scrawl I knew so well were two messages—two, in the whole time I'd been gone! One was just a number, one digit too short, as if he'd been too tired to write the whole thing out. The other message, marked, "Important! Call back!" was from a local health spa offering a free analysis of body fat.

"That jerk," I muttered.

"Don't put Daddy down," Cass said calmly, slipping into a chair at the kitchen table beside me. "He doesn't put you down."

"Of course he does." I showed Cass the newspaper articles he'd cut out and saved for me. One was about a woman just my age who had single-handedly stopped the destruction of ten thousand acres of rainforest. Another gave new evidence that Joan of Arc was a man. Two were about AIDS, and one was about cigarettes causing facial wrinkles. "He just does it in a way no one but I can understand," I explained. I was remembering the birthday card he'd sent last month. It showed a woman in a black cloak walking toward the edge of a cliff. Inside he'd written, in pencil, "Hope some of your dreams come true," and I'd ripped it from corner to corner, thinking, *All* my dreams are going to come true, and they're not dreams, you fool, they are real choices in a real world and they are going to happen because I'm going to make them happen, and they are going to happen *soon*.

I lit the first cigarette I'd wanted since I'd been home and exhaled, staring out the kitchen window. It was strange to see my own backyard, and again I had the feeling that I wasn't really home yet, that Alejandra or her mother or one of the other volunteers would be walking in any second, talking to me in a language I did not understand, asking for help I could not give. I glanced at Cass. "He didn't see that article that called me a 'heroine' did he?" Cass half-shrugged and ducked her head. "Good," I said. "Because he would have used it to line the rat's cage with."

"Mom." Cass was shocked, I knew, because the only time she calls me Mom is when I'm not acting like one. I stubbed my cigarette out; I felt ashamed. After all, peace begins at home; that's what I tell everyone I talk to, and it's true, too, in some homes at least. I turned my hand toward Cass, palm up. "I'm sorry," I said. I could see her pet rat's cage in the corner; it was lined, appropriately, with the front page of the *New York Times*. "I overreacted. And anyway," I remembered, "it wasn't the paper that called me a heroine, it was your teacher."

"She said everyone should live by their values like you do," Cass said.

"She did?" Again I felt a rush of pleasure, followed by a rush of doubt. If I were truly living by my values, I thought, I wouldn't be sitting here picking on Cass, who is innocent and undefended and my favorite person in the world. If I were truly living by my values I'd be doing something to right the wrongs I make myself. I reached into my shirt pocket and pulled out the piece of sugarcane I'd bought her at the market that morning. Cass took it dutifully and took a few tentative licks at the piece I cut off for her.

"What was it like down there?" she asked, after a while.

"Just like here," I said. "Only with people trying to kill you."

Cass waited, patient, and after a second I started to talk. I talked about the young boys in uniform, so playful and shy you think they're joking, and then you notice their carbines. About the flatbed truck full of men with their hands tied behind their backs, and about the spotted dog that chased that truck, howling, through six blocks of traffic. I talked about the soldiers I'd seen at the beach, patrolling the empty waves, and about the white pig in the Mendoza's front yard, and the bombed out schoolhouse and the bombed out hospital, and the shops full of car parts and Barbie dolls I'd seen in the city. I talked about Alejandra, a girl her age who had tuberculosis, a disease Cass had never heard of, and about Alejandra's mother, who claimed to see "spirits" when she prayed, the spirits of all the people in her village who had disappeared.

Cass listened, intent. She is a wonderful listener, so different from her father, and she asks all the right questions—questions, that is, I can't answer. "Why can't people," she asked, "just be nicer to each other? Why can't we all get along?"

"I don't know," I told her. "You'd think it would be so simple, but it's not."

Cass nodded and yawned. It was getting dark and we were both tired. She politely disposed of the sugarcane, gave me a goodnight hug, and went to bed, and I peeled off my filthy jeans and went to the bathroom to take a long shower.

The bathroom looked as unfamiliar as the rest of the house, too big by far, and faintly unclean, and cluttered with things we didn't need. The shower floor had that sticky tar-like substance on it that he used to bring home on his skin from the shop, so I knew he'd at least washed once or twice. I thought of him standing here, naked, in the same space where I stood, with his eyes closed and the water beating down and his bare feet where my feet were, and it gave me the creeps. I saw one of his brown hairs, thin as a spider leg, stuck to the wall, and I aimed the shower at it to hose it down. I wanted every last trace of him out of my house. I turned the water off, glad to step out. As I toweled my hair I noticed a bottle of perfume on the counter, an old bottle of musk stuff I used to wear when we were first married. I sniffed it, curious. Was that what I'd smelled when I first came in the house? Did he wear my perfume when I was gone?

I frowned at the bottle, troubled. It brought back a time I don't think of often, when we were living like gypsies, he and I, traveling up and down the coast in a beat-up old van, picking apples and strawberries, sleeping on beaches, fighting even then, of course, but talking. We did a lot of talking in those years, before he decided to start his own business, before I decided to go back to school, before we had Cass. We did a lot of laughing, and I miss that sometimes, the way we used to roar at each other. Now when he laughs it's this silent wheeze, as if someone had just punched him in the stomach, and he only laughs at the bad news—my car being towed from the protest at the Naval Yard delighted him for days and the power failure the time I was being interviewed live on the radio.

I put the perfume down, pulled on a robe, and went back to the kitchen to see if he'd left any wine. As I passed the guest room I glanced in. The bed was untouched, the curtains were drawn, and the note I'd left to thank him for staying with Cass was still tucked, unread, under the vase where the roses and poppies had dried on their stalks. He never once took what I had to offer, I thought. He never liked the food I cooked or the books I read or the friends I brought home. He wasn't interested in the classes I went to or the papers I wrote or the ideas that made me want to shout all night. "It's such an act," he'd say, when I'd come home late, flushed and hoarse from one of the meetings. "You're such a fake." And his eyes, when he looked at me then from his place on the couch, were almost wide open, almost alive. Then they'd hood again, and he'd turn from me.

I picked up the vase, crumpled the note, and went into the kitchen. The garbage bag was full of ale bottles and pizza boxes and losing lottery tickets and TV listings. I made some instant coffee. I'd lived on nothing but coffee for weeks, it seemed, and I was used to it; it didn't even keep me awake anymore. As I stirred in the honey the phone rang. It was Greg. He was three hundred miles away, at another conference, and I could hear a woman laughing and two men arguing behind him. "Hey," he said, sounding far-off and rushed, "How was your time down there? I want to hear all about it. But maybe when I get back, OK? Right now I just wanted you to know there's a special on TV tonight about the Sandinistas."

"OK," I said. "I'll watch it. And Greg? A professional question? What would you think of a man who got into a woman's perfume?"

"I'd think he wanted to be close to her in some way," Greg said. "Got to run. I'll call." He blew me a kiss and hung up.

Close to me? I carried my coffee to the couch and sat down. The pillows reeked of that old musk stuff and I pushed them away, sickened. The way to be close to me is to talk to me, and let me talk back, and to touch me, and let me reach out. He couldn't do that; he didn't know how. The only thing he could do was lie on this couch, night after night, and push me away when I got too close. "Can you stand somewhere else?" he'd said once, when I was trying to tell him about an article I was trying to write. "You're blocking the light."

"That's not *light*," I pointed out. "That's the TV. Don't you know the difference?"

"No," he drawled, dumb, "I don't know the difference. I'm just the bozo who brings home the bacon. You know the difference. Right? So why don't you tell me—like you tell everyone else, over and over, on and on, all the time. Why don't you help me understand the great big world?" he asked. "Why don't you change my life?"

His life. I remembered something Alejandra's mother had asked me. "Do you think," she had asked, "we make our own lives?" And I'd answered, No, how could we?—for I was thinking of her, and the horrible things that had happened to her, none of them her fault or her choice. But what about him? Look how he lives. He still sleeps in the shop. He started to sleep there before he moved out, and he hasn't moved since. He has a television there, of course, a huge color set, and a mattress on the floor in back. He has a refrigerator with nothing in it, and a hot plate he doesn't bother to use. He has some of Cass's artwork on the walls, and a photo of the three of us at Disneyland when she was six, and a calendar that still shows snow. He's alone most of the day and most of the night. He meets women in bars, and there was one girl, an aerobics instructor, who lasted almost three months. "She had problems," he said—which means, of course, she had life, she had hope, she had moved on. He has no men friends outside the shop. He sees Cass once a week, on Sunday afternoons, and they go to the movies; Cass says he sleeps. He's lost twenty pounds and still wears that old blue jacket with the grease stain on the cuff. He won't see a therapist or get involved in a support group; when I suggest these things he just stares at me, his eyes bright with thoughts he finds very funny.

I sat my coffee cup down with a bang on the table and reached for the remote control, wiping it first on my robe. I clicked on the set. There was the end of some comedy show: stupid. Then one of those wrestling matches he used to watch all the time: stupid stupid. Then the news: stupid stupid stupid. Then the show Greg wanted me to see. Some liar from Associated Press was asking some liar from the Pentagon all the wrong questions and getting all the wrong answers and despite myself I started to drift off. My head kept getting heavier and heavier and I could feel myself fade.

I had this image—not a dream exactly, just an image that kept getting bigger and bigger. It was something I'd seen down there, from the bus, when we were driving through cane fields. It was a turkey vulture, tall and black and ugly the way vultures are, with their bare red necks and bald heads, and it was sitting on a fence post hunched over watching something in the dirt below. "Look," the man beside me had said, "he's waiting for his dinner to die," and we'd shivered and talked about other things, and I hadn't thought about that bird again, but now it appeared to me, familiar and close, and I realized it was perched on the edge of the couch. It was peering down, patient, waiting for me to get tired and give up. I wanted to, too. The conference—I could never tell Greg this—but the conference hadn't accomplished a thing. Alejandra was still dying, her mother was seeing new spirits every day, the baby boys were still aiming their deadly toys. What's the point? I thought. What makes me think I can make any difference? I'm as weak and shallow and false as he said I was. The vulture bent close and I hated him so I jerked up with a start. My head was buzzing and my throat was dry and my legs were numb, but I got to my feet, and even though I knew I was being what he used to call "ridiculous," I watched the rest of that damn show with my arms crossed, standing up, and when that jerk from the Pentagon said, "This is not a war, see, what we have down here is not a war, it's what we call a 'low intensity conflict,'" I hooted so hard that I woke Cass up and she came trailing out, still wearing the embroidered shirt I'd brought her, stumbling a little with sleep as she put her arms around me, saying, "Come to bed now, Mom. You're home."

Leaving the Colonel

SHE COULDN'T LEAVE HIM; she had nothing to wear. She was wearing rubber thongs and her fat dress, and her fat dress was stained under the arms and ripped at the seams and besides it was a dress she'd made herself about five hundred years ago when puffed sleeves were in. She couldn't leave wearing something she'd made herself. It was one thing to slop around the kitchen looking like a Before Picture, but it was another to walk out the front door and down the block and across the world in full view. No thanks. When she was ready to leave, she was leaving in style; she was leaving in ranch mink and diamonds, with her hair piled high and something in her suitcase besides bunion pads and size sixteens.

And when, the interviewer said, do you expect this fashion event to occur?

He stepped into the kitchen, guiding the cord of his microphone around the dirty plates stacked on the floor.

I said, When I'm ready.

The interviewer pushed back one cuff and glanced at his wristwatch. You've been talking about leaving the colonel for twenty years, he said.

You think I can't leave him? I can leave him, my dear. I can leave him like that.

She snapped her fingers. Tap water sprayed from her hand and freckled the interviewer's powder blue coat. She smiled and took another sip from the teacup filled with bourbon she kept behind the toaster.

Nothing gets older, the interviewer said, than an old threat.

Threat schmet. That's a promise, my friend. Leaving the colonel is a promise I made to myself the minute I married him, so don't think you can change my mind at this late date. Twenty years, she said, my foot.

The interviewer sighed, lifted the garbage bag off the seat of his favorite chair, sat down, and crossed his long legs. She glared at him an instant and then, relieved, she smiled. Twenty years could not possibly have passed because the interviewer looked exactly the same as the first day she'd met him. He'd been thin and snippy then and he was thin and snippy still. He still had the pegged pants, the blue sports coat, the suede shoes with plaid laces; he still yawned in her face and he still bit his nails. His hair was still crimped in oiled blond waves, there were no lines by his lips, and his cheeks, although sallow, were as smooth as a boy's. She reached out to touch him, but, as always, he ducked away. Her fingers touched air.

Hot air, she said fondly. That's what you're full of.

Not me, said the interviewer, and his voice was so gloomy she glanced at him again. I'm not the one who's been saying I'm going to begin a new life, make something of myself.

But I am going to leave, she corrected him. And I've been thinking a lot about my future career. I've been thinking I might teach domestic arts at a high school—teach all those young girls how to take a decent normal life and chop it and mop it and slop it to bits. Or I might join the circus. Or I might join the army—ha!—and court-martial the colonel. There's nothing I can't do once I decide to do it, right?

She grinned at him, but he was sucking a hangnail and did not grin back. She shrugged and concentrated on her work. She was rinsing the wild blackberries she'd picked early that morning. As she shook the colander back and forth she noticed for the first time that many of the berries were red, many were bright green, and some still had their prickly stems attached. She was not surprised. She had asked the colonel a hundred times to plant a real garden in back—the kind of garden her father had planted when she was a child, an old-fashioned vegetable garden with curly lettuce and sweet red carrots and berries trained to a trellis—but oh, no, the colonel heard nothing she said, did nothing she wanted, sat all day and all night in front of his television with the light from the screen flickering over his pistol. Was it any wonder she had to wander through the woods like a beggar just to find a few fresh berries? Was it any wonder she was a deeply unhappy, disappointed woman?

Men have let me down, she said. Since my father died nothing's gone right. My sons are both pansies, my husband's a tyrant, and you, look at you, the biggest letdown of all: a talk show host who never talks.

I talk, the interviewer said.

Shut up. It's my show, remember? Just tell me why I'm stuck on this stupid show in this stupid house in the middle of nowhere. Tell me why I'm the only woman in the world who's too fat to wear anything she owns but a torn pink dress with puffed sleeves she had to make herself. Tell me why I slave all day. Tell me why I suffer.

You could change.

I cannot change.

You could try.

I hate my clothes, she said.

I don't think clothes are the issue. I think...

What do you know about issues, asshole?

That felt good. She drained the teacup and started to say it again but her heart wasn't in it. Why pick on him? He was just doing his job. Her job was to make little messes and then clean them up, but his job was tough too.

Just joking, she said. You know me. Ha ha. Always joking.

He wouldn't answer. She had hurt his feelings. She refilled the teacup to the brim from the bourbon bottle, reached for the sugar bag, dumped the berries and sugar together into a pot, and set the pot on the stove with a bang.

You take yourself too seriously, she said. You look like a pompous old judge sitting up there in your chair. So silent and stuck up. Guess what I'm cooking for you, old judgy-pudgy? Come on. Guess. I'm cooking your favorite. Blackberry jelly. Oh, boy. Yum yum. Blackberry jelly. It's the hottest damn day of the year and every other woman in the world is lolling around the swim club guzzling gin and tonics, but I'm in the kitchen cooking blackberry jelly for you, my friend judgy, and for my husband the colonel. Don't you want to know why?

The interviewer looked up. His eyes were guarded and hostile. The microphone lay loose in his palm. No, he said. Why?

Because you hate it, she said. Because if there's one thing in the whole world you hate and the colonel hates it's blackberry jelly. Oh, laugh. Come on. All your troubles disappear when you laugh. Ha ha. See? No more troubles. What are you staring at now?

He was looking at the teacup in her hand.

Do you like the design? Do you like the bridge, and the bough, and the little painted birdie?

Yes, the interviewer said. I do.

Tweet tweet goes the birdie.

I always have, the interviewer said. He mopped his brow with the tip of his tie and looked around the kitchen. But wasn't there a saucer that matched the cup? Wasn't there a creamer and a little pot?

There was, tweet tweet, a little pot.

What happened to those?

Smashed. She leaned forward so he could smell her breath. Smashed. Smashed. Smashed.

Well that's a shame, the interviewer said, turning aside. You had nice things and you broke them.

Oh, I ruin everything, she agreed. And what I don't ruin, the colonel does.

The smell of burnt fruit filled the room.

See? she cried. I hate that man!

She opened a window and waved to a neighbor, using each finger. The neighbor looked up but did not wave back.

Sometimes I think what I better do is give up and kill myself and that goes for him too.

The interviewer said nothing.

I'm talking about getting it over with, she said. I'm talking about ending it all. I'm talking about serious stuff and you're sitting there staring off into space with your doodad lying on your lap like some little kid who wants to play with himself but doesn't know how.

The interviewer flushed and closed his fist around the microphone.

It's going to be a pretty sorry show today if you don't snap out of it, she said.

About the show...

Oh, screw the show. I'm sick of the show. Every damn day the colonel sits in there watching TV and you sit in here asking me the same old questions: When are you going to leave him? How are you going to leave him? Let's examine the issues. Etcetera. Etcetera. Who listens? Who cares? No one, that's who. So why go on? Why continue to broadcast my innermost thoughts to the rest of the world? Because let me tell you a secret. Can I tell you a secret? I've never cared about the world. And the world's never cared about me. Now you know my secret. But then you know all my secrets. You are not a perfect person, not by any means. But I'll say one thing for you: you listen.

It's my job to listen.

Job schwob. It's your duty.

The interviewer flushed again but said nothing.

Your duty, she repeated, as she dreamily stirred the pot over the flames, is to listen and learn and eventually laugh. I can always laugh at myself, ha ha, and then I feel better. Do you want to know a secret about this morning? Do you want to make me feel better?

I don't care, the interviewer muttered.

What? Put down that microphone. This isn't for the show. This is off the record. This is for you. Are you listening? Good. Now this morning it was hot. It was hot, I was tired, I wanted to leave him. He was in his chair, watching cartoons, clicking his teeth, pointing his pistol. I thought, Yes, I will leave him. I got as far as the swim club when something caught my eye—berries, blackberries—growing by the side of the road. You know me, how impulsive I am. I started to pick them. I remembered how my father used to fill his hat with treasures—treasures, he called them, treasures for me. Of course I don't have a decent hat so I had to use the bag I keep my knitting in. I ruined my knitting. I ruined my dress. I ruined the bag. I scratched my arms and got blood on my ankles. Once I lost my balance and sat right down on a patch of poison oak. I sat on the patch thinking: What am I doing? Am I crazy or what? Is this funny or what? The sun was so hot and so white in the sky and I felt invisible and old, much older than I really am, and I could hear splashing and laughing from the swim club and cars going fast and the beat beat beat of my stupid heart and everything sounded far away, especially my own stupid heart and my own stupid voice saying Father Father, and I wanted to lie down and go to sleep, right there, but then I remembered our show this afternoon and I knew I had to get back right away. I knew you'd be wanting to ask me some questions and I knew our listeners would be wanting some answers. And so far today—do you know what?—so far today you've asked me hardly one question.

She shook the jelly spoon at him. Hot drops spattered across the floor. Ask me a question!

What were you knitting?

Knitting? I almost died out there of heat stroke and it's the colonel's fault I don't have a hat, and you ask about knitting? Well I'll tell you what I was knitting. I was knitting a cozy. A cozy for the colonel's little pistol. Now ask me another.

What color was it?

Color? Well what do you know. Another good question. The color was...

At that moment the colonel walked into the kitchen. He was a small red-faced man with a bald head and eyelashes as long and thick as a girl's. He went to the sink, cleared a space, poured a glass of water, and drank it.

He smiled at her as he wiped his lips. He smiled at the interviewer too. She thought about introducing the two men but, after all this time, decided against it. She watched as the colonel poured the rest of the glass into his pistol, which was a water pistol, plastic. She watched as he capped it.

It was white, she said. Only now it looks like it's been in an accident, because of the stains. Can you hear what I'm saying?

Nope, said the colonel. What are you saying?

He smiled again and left the room.

She turned toward the interviewer. As I mentioned before, you are by no means a perfect person but at least you have the decency to listen. You at least wait for my answers.

Twenty years, the interviewer agreed. Twenty years I've waited for answers.

Twenty schwenty. Ask some more questions. Ask your old questions.

When are you leaving?

As soon as I can.

Where will you go?

As far as I'm able.

How will you do it?

On my knees if I have to.

Why?

What?

Why?

You've never asked that before.

Yes I have. That's the one I've asked you every day for twenty years.

Because I'm not happy, she said after a moment. I'm not happy with the colonel.

Perhaps you wouldn't be happy anyway. Perhaps if you left him you'd feel just as bad. You might feel worse, even, than you do now. Have you ever thought of that? You might end up in that room.

What room?

The room you told me about.

What room? That room? Ha! That room by the river with the hot sun slanting through the blinds and the paper peeling off the walls and the empty bottle dropping from my hand and rolling bumpety bump across the floor?

Yes.

Well that room came from some movie I saw as a kid. That, and there's the other one, the room full of loonies standing around laughing at me— both those rooms came from the movies. They're not real. They're not going to happen. They're just scenes from some movie my father took me to years ago, when I was a kid. One thing you don't know. I was happy, when I was a kid.

You've told me.

What?

You've told me and told me.

I wish you'd leave that hangnail alone; are you nervous or what? If you'd take your hands out of your mouth and sit up straight and stop being nervous I could tell you a few things about a man you ought to know something about and I do mean my father. My father was a gentleman. My father told me—he told me that one day I'd be famous. A famous star, that's what he said. He said I had the looks and the personality, all I needed was the luck. Well you know me. You know my luck. The colonel came along and that was that. I left my father and for what. For this luckless life with the colonel.

I don't know why you always blame the colonel.

Who do you want me to blame? You? Shall I blame you? Let's talk about you—you know what you are? You are...my friend. Yes you are. Come on, give me a smile. You are my friend, my very best friend. Is that the smile of someone's best friend? Don't you have a better smile than that? Why if it weren't for you, I would have left the colonel years ago. I had my suitcase packed, remember? My ticket reserved, my sons in my arms; I was going to try to find my father. And as I walked out the front door you walked in the back. Where are you going? you asked. Just like that you said it, as if you had a right to know: Now where are you going?

I'm leaving, said the interviewer.

So I said I was leaving, and you said, Relax. Sit down. Have a drink. Let's look at some issues.

Well, said the interviewer. He cleared his throat. Times have changed. I'll say.

She smiled, shook her head, wiped her hands down the front of her dress, and stared at the pot of berries still boiling on the stove. What was I making? she asked. Some sort of pie?

Times have changed, the interviewer repeated in a louder voice. And I have changed too.

She glanced at him. No you haven't, she said. It's very peculiar but the truth is you haven't changed a bit.

I have changed, the interviewer insisted. I have changed inside. He stood. I have grown, he said. I have developed as a person.

She stirred the pot, musing. I used to think that if I ever left the colonel

I would have to go straight to that room by the river like some convict going straight to a jail cell but now I know better, now I know I wasn't making a pie, I was making jelly, jelly for the colonel, what a waste of effort, what a waste of time; the colonel can't tell jelly from jam, he lives in a dream. I could walk out the door this second and he'd never miss me or know I was gone, so why do I bother, why do I try?

Please listen, the interviewer said. Please stop saying the same things over and over and listen to me. I have something to tell you. Something important.

She looked at him.

I'm leaving the show, the interviewer said. I'm leaving you and I'm leaving the colonel and I'm leaving right now.

You can't, she said.

I have to. Don't smile. Don't smile at me. Don't laugh at me.

I can't help it, she said. You look so funny standing there. You look so funny standing there with your face squinched up, in those ugly old clothes.

The interviewer glanced down at the front of his jacket. He straightened his tie and flecked some sugar off his shoes. I look all right, he said.

You look like a clown. You look like a horror story. How can you leave, looking like that? It's not Halloween, you know; it's not even near it. You know what I'd do if I were you? I'd sit down. I'd have a drink. I'd have another. And then I'd examine the issues. What are the issues?

I'm dissatisfied with the way my life has turned out, the interviewer said. I'm tired of doing the same old show in the same old style year after year with you.

That's one.

Things inside me are crying out. My heart feels too big to stay locked in this jacket. My voice gets caught in the knot of my tie. I want to taste and touch and test the world. I want to try myself and see where my talents take me. I want to be free.

That's two.

I feel if I don't leave now something might happen and I might never be able to leave you at all.

That's three.

That's all, I guess. He paused. Aren't you going to wish me luck?

Don't ask me for luck. That's one thing I can't give.

Well good-bye then. He walked toward the door, turned, and stopped. You could come with me, he said.

No thanks. I don't want to go where you're going. I don't want to go there at all. Have you forgotten what's waiting out there?

He followed her eyes toward the door. Life, he said.

Life schnife. There's nothing out there but a room. A room by a river. Waiting for you, my friend, waiting for you.

I'm going to enroll in a university, the interviewer said. I'm going to go into video, that's the new thing now, that's the coming thing, video. I'm going to fall in love with a red-headed girl and make red-headed babies. I'm going to travel to Spain and New Guinea. I'm going to buy a sports car and take a trip by hot air balloon and learn Chinese and take tap dancing lessons. You made that room up, he added.

That's not all I made up.

What do you mean?

I made you up, mister. That's what I mean. Don't act as if you didn't know. Look at your hair, look at your clothes, listen to yourself. You're mine, mister.

No I'm not.

Mine, mister.

Mister who, then? The interviewer wheeled around and glared at her. If you made me up, he said, if you've botched me like you've botched everything else you've ever made, then tell me my name. You don't even know my name, he said.

I know your name. I've always known your name.

What is it? The interviewer watched her carefully to see if she was going to trick him. When he was sure she was not, he unwound the cord and raised the microphone to her lips. This would be her last answer.

Asshole, she said. Mr. Jerk Stupid Asshole Junior. That is your name.

When she looked up from laughing he was gone. Well go and good riddance, she cried. She swirled the last drop of bourbon in her cup. She had so much to do today! She had the kitchen to clean and dinner to cook and the kitchen to clean and breakfast to cook and the kitchen to clean and this jelly to cook. She lifted the pot and poured some of the dark liquid into a jar. It tasted sour and smelled burnt and ran as fast as a river; it hadn't jelled, hadn't begun to. She could either boil it again or she could serve it as syrup, or she could give it to the colonel to fill his little pistol with—whatever she decided to do, it would be the wrong decision because all her decisions all her life had been wrong wrong wrong, but it was too late to start thinking about that now; it was very late indeed and she was very tired indeed. What she wanted to do right now was lie down on that place beneath the window where the sun came through the blinds and made quiet bars on the floor. She wanted to pretend that the bottle she was carrying toward that warm bright place was the hand of her father as he led her through a garden of roses and cherries and heavy ripe plums—she wanted to sleep for a second and when she awoke she would have a good laugh at herself, her stupid fat self passed out on the floor like some old wino in some hotel, yes that's what she'd do and then she would leave him.

Talking to Strangers

I KNOW THIS IS RUDE. I know you don't know me. At first I thought you might have seen my name in the papers, but I can tell by your frown that my name means nothing. That's all right. My name doesn't matter. It was a simple girl's name, like yours, not much to it except the MD at the end, which I felt gave it weight. Perhaps you saw the photograph? The reporters chose one my parents kept on their mantel; it was taken the same year I started at Mercy Hospital. It shows me with my glasses off and my hair curled down around my shoulders. It doesn't look a thing like me. I never smiled with my lips clamped shut like that. I smiled like you were smiling a second ago, before you heard me call you; I smiled with lots of teeth and gums showing and my nose wrinkled up. I dressed like you, too, in blue jeans and T-shirt, and I pulled my hair back in a braid when I hiked.

I used to hike on the mountain though. You can see where I went if you turn and walk backward. The Ridge Trail is up there, against the clouds. I often looked down on this beach, but I never thought of coming here until I saw you walking across it today. Now I see what a nice beach it is, brown and windblown and so deserted it almost seems private. Your own place for your own thoughts; that's hard to find sometimes, I know. But you've found it here. I am impressed. Solitude. Privacy. You can run along the shore here, or turn somersaults, or take your clothes off, or talk out loud. You're talking now. You're saying "help." You're saying "help" in a low voice, looking from side to side, half-smiling as if this is all very funny.

Which it probably is. I'll grant you that. The minute I saw you I almost laughed too. There you were, striding straight toward me, your sandals in one hand, your lunch in the other. You looked preoccupied, and pleased with yourself too, as if you had just made a private, important decision. Perhaps you had just decided to change jobs, or live in Europe, or go back to school, or have a baby. I had decided, the day I hiked up the mountain, to marry Fran Silvera.

Fran knew me, or said he did, like the back of his hand. He had known from the first day we started to work together at Mercy that I'd be his wife. I had skin like his mother's, a laugh like his sister's, legs like his first grade teacher's. I was the right woman for him, Fran decided. I was the woman he wanted to marry.

He proposed at the hospital. It wasn't romantic. We had paused in our rounds and were standing at the window on the seventh floor, looking out. Fran's arm was around my waist and his voice was low and persistent against my ear but his face was turned aside. I followed his gaze and saw the mountain in the distance, a far blue shape with the sun setting behind it. I don't want to rush you, Fran said. I'll give you all the time you want. Just tell me tomorrow.

He touched my arm and then he walked away. I knew his walk so well, that quick crooked walk with the head bent, one hand in a pocket. I loved his walk. It was jaunty and purposeful, like Fran himself. Yet I wanted him to stop. I wanted him to stop and turn and come back and look at me. He didn't, of course. He disappeared down the hall.

That night I thought of a lot of good reasons not to marry Fran. The first reason was my friend Elaine—Elaine who says she will get back into medicine as soon as her children are in school. The second was Bett—Bett who left her own practice to follow her husband to Africa, and who writes how proud she is, of his research. The third was Nina—Nina who opened a clinic with her husband in the country, and who now does her share of the practice, plus the paperwork, cooking, gardening, and carpentry. I remembered the contempt in Nina's voice the last time she talked about the husband she used to worship.

I thought of these friends—good doctors married to good doctors— and I thought of Fran's back disappearing down the hall, and I longed for some clean vast windy space where I could walk and breathe and see things clearly. The next morning I put on my hiking boots, braided my hair, dropped a lunch in my day pack, and drove out to the mountain.

It was a day like today, mild and oddly empty. The sky was cloudy but the sun felt warm, and I could feel the skin on my face, throat, and hands begin to tighten as I climbed. I walked fast and was halfway up the Ridge Trail before I began to notice the world around me. The first thing I saw was a jay feather, dropped like an arrow on the path. It was a slim, soft, bright blue feather. It might have been an omen, but even now I don't see how; it was just a lovely thing to find, and I picked it up and wove it through my braid. The mountain lilac was beginning to bud against the pines, and I could see drifts of acacia in the ravines far below. In another month, I thought, the wild iris will be in bloom—I'll bring Fran then; I'll show him this trail. I imagined Fran hiking beside me, matching breath for breath, step for step; I imagined his pleasure in the deer prints, wild mushrooms, and clumps of wood violets I could point out. He would like it here, with me, I thought; he'd look where I looked and see as I do. The idea of his hand in mine as I climbed felt close, and comforting, and right. I am not like my friends, I reminded myself. I am not Bett, or Nina, or Elaine; I am me. The small word *me* exploded, as it can, and for a second I felt splashed with light—jubilant—wild and strong and sure of myself. I will marry Fran, I thought. I will have his children and I will have my own career as well. I will have it all, I thought. I saw my future streak between the clouds, and as I grinned the sun came out; I thought it came for me. I turned the final wide cliff-side curve of the trail and stopped, overwhelmed as always by the view of city, bridge, and bay that met me.

Everything shimmered, grey on grey, quiet and distant. I could pick Mercy out from the other buildings in the city skyline; it looked large, even from the mountaintop. I took the jay feather from my hair and waved it toward the windows on the seventh floor. If Fran were staring out the glass at the mountain now, he'd see me dancing, shouting *Yes*. I wrote Y-E-S in the air with my feather; I was about to underline it and add an exclamation point when I heard another word behind me. One word. Hello.

I turned and for a long time I saw nothing at all. My heart was racing and my glasses had slipped and I was still smiling; you know how it is. At last I saw a sight so simple, almost comic, that I can't forget it: two feet in jogging shoes sticking out from behind a toyon tree. Someone has followed me, I thought. I tried to recall if I had seen anyone on the trail, but I could remember seeing no one, hearing no one; there had been scarcely more than two or three cars in the lot when I'd parked. I shivered and then I thought: dumb. This is just some guy taking a solitary piss behind the bushes; he's talking to himself, not me. Courteously, to let him know he wasn't alone, I began to hum. I had been ready to burst into "The Wedding March" a moment before. It seemed inappropriate now. I thought a second and began to hum a fight song from college football games.

The shoes didn't move. They were new, blue, two-tone shoes, size ten or eleven, with bright white laces. I should have screamed then, right away. I should have stopped humming and I should have taken a deep breath and hollered out with all my might. Perhaps it wouldn't have done any good. The only other hikers at that time were little boys on a Cub Scout outing, looking for lizards. I am glad they didn't hear me, and I am glad they didn't find me later. All my work with children and children's bodies would have been ruined forever if children had been the ones to find my body, scattered like a bag of kicked garbage among the damp leaves.

For of course that's what happened; you've known that all along; even if you don't read the papers, you know what the world's like, and the minute you heard my voice you knew I was going to tell you a story you've heard a thousand times before. You duck your head and turn your collar up to deafen my voice. That's all right; I'll raise my voice. I raised it then. "Hello yourself," I said.

"Hello," he repeated. He stepped out from behind the tree. He was just a boy, no older than twenty, with a smooth round rosy face. There was a light in his eyes that made him beautiful, at first—he looked so glad to see me, so radiant he shone. The gun trembled in his hand and his lips trembled too, from smiling. I could see he was crazy; crazy was scribbled in the curly blond hair he'd hacked short all around his skull and in the marks like war paint he'd put on his cheeks, but his smile made me think, for a minute, he might be harmless. Then the smile disappeared. His lips puckered, his eyes muddied, he looked ready to cry. He's disappointed, I thought. He's been waiting for someone else, another girl, not me. I'm not who he thought I was. From the back, perhaps, as he was following me, from the back he saw my braid and it made him think I was the woman he wanted, but now that he sees I am Me and not Her—now, I thought, that he knows he is wrong— well, he will let me go. I let out a sigh and I think I nodded a little as I started to edge away. I meant to turn and race into the woods. I meant to escape. Later I would tell Fran Silvera and our children about this mad boy I'd met once, and how I'd outwitted him. I nodded again. I thought if the boy saw I was not much older than he, and wore blue jeans like he did—if he saw who I was, a doctor for God's sake, and a girl—if he saw all that, he would like me. Men have always liked me.

But this boy didn't like me. He didn't even see me. I can describe the way he looked, with those circles and zigzags painted onto his face; I can describe the way he spoke, in a small clear voice, accentless; I can draw an exact replica of his one gold earring and map the moles on his throat. I saw him so well. But he didn't see me. When he told me to take my clothes off he might have been talking to the air itself. "Who do you think you are?" I asked. I wheeled and ran. He grabbed me then; it was so easy; he was faster than I thought, and strong. He hit me as a man would hit another man, hard, in the face with the butt of his pistol. I fell back screaming. My screams were so thin and so high they seemed to come from someone else, not me— perhaps they came from the woman he wanted, for he smiled again as he knelt on my neck. Then he shoved the gun barrel deep into my mouth. I could feel my teeth chip on the metal; my mouth flooded with blood; I gagged and could not swallow.

"You know who I am," he said. "I'm your master. I want you to say that. I want to hear the word *master.*"

"Monster," I said, my mouth full of blood.

"Again."

And this time—can you hear me say it?—this time I spit and started to cry, and said, of course, "Master."

He nodded, satisfied, and sat back on his heels. I was praying he'd rape me. I was praying he'd rape me and beat me and leave me alive, and I could crawl down the mountain at night and have my teeth fixed and everything would be all right. So when he yanked off my day pack and told me again to take off my clothes, I did—not seductively, no, I wouldn't give him that— but I took them off, crying, my T-shirt and my jeans and my shoes and my underpants and my glasses. He threw my day pack into the trees, jabbed my arm with his gun, and nudged me step by step off the trail and into the woods; we stopped by a little creek and he made me lie down there, on the rocks.

If he had touched me with his body I might be living now, for there is reprieve in even the roughest touch; skin on skin has its own way of bonding. But he touched me with his gun. Here, there, like I would touch a patient with a stethoscope, only never would I touch a patient as lovelessly as he touched me. I lay like a patient, staring straight up. Without my glasses I could scarcely see his face, but I could see the pale blue sky, caught between the bare branches of the trees, and I could hear the cold little sounds of the creek, and the boy's quiet breathing as he examined me with his gun. I had the jay feather hidden inside my hand and as the boy's round unblinking eye came toward my face I clenched it tight. Just as he jabbed his gun between my legs and forced it up, I lunged. The jay feather fell from his cheek, harmless as a tear, and I fell too, fell out of myself, tumbled loose, free as air. Even if I had been rescued at that instant I don't think I would have known how to come back inside my body. By the time the gun, unconcerned, pulled out to probe a pulse at my breast I was changed, dead forever, and already talking—for I was talking steadily the whole time. I was begging for my life.

"Let me go," I was saying, "and I'll never tell anyone this happened; I'll do anything for you; I'll be your slave if that's what you want; I'll give you money; you can live at my house; you can have my car; I'll never betray you; I'll never tell them I know you; I'll say I've never seen you before in my life."

The boy wasn't listening. He was nodding to a rhythm I couldn't hear, maybe the rhythm of my own words. I was telling him I was a doctor by then; I was promising free treatment. I was saying I could help him, change his life, save him. And he? He just said, "Roll over."

I did. I rolled over and closed my eyes against the stones and then I opened them again and saw where a single spot of sun had fallen on my wristwatch. I could not see the time, and when I raised my head he put his foot on my head and drove the gun up my rectum; before I could catch my breath he pulled the gun out and held it close to my nose with his own nose wrinkled, as if the smell of my body ought to disgust me. It did not disgust me. Poor body, I thought. I started to stand. I started to walk away. I was never going to Fran Silvera, I knew that; I wasn't a girl Fran knew anymore. I wasn't a girl anyone knew anymore. And yet I was still myself. More myself than I had ever been, and this seemed strange, to be so complete and so unknown. Poor Fran, I thought. He had not seen me before and he would not see me again. Nobody would. I felt sorry about that, but mostly I felt tired. I had been talking to strangers, for such a long time, to so little purpose. "Who do you think *you* are?" the boy shouted and before I could answer he shot me, just once, in the face, and that's all it took; there's no trick to dying, not when you're tired.

It wasn't until after I'd died he remembered the knife; in that, I was lucky. He is called The Scalp Hunter in the papers now, and there is speculation that he grew up on an Indian reservation down south; I wouldn't know about that. He took the top of my head off and looked inside, and then he slit my sternum and parted the muscles back like ragged red tent curtains. He was delicate, swift, intent, and scared. He was looking for Her, I think. He was looking for that other woman, and he thought she might be inside me, hiding.

He didn't find her there, though. He hasn't found her anywhere, not yet. He's looking. The sheriff's men are looking too. They found the other two women on the mountain after they found me; they think I was left beside the trail deliberately, to lead the way to the other two bodies. I wouldn't mind thinking that was true; I'd like to be useful, but what can I do? No one can hear me. No one can see me. The memory of my laughter shakes my parents awake, terrified, at midnight; my name is a warning to schoolgirls. My friends crowd over coffee in a neighbor's apartment; they laugh at themselves because they are afraid to take my key, open my door, and confront my things: my bedroom slippers, my tennis racket, my turquoise bracelets, my tin of jasmine tea. These are just *things*, my friends explain to my neighbor. Yet they fear these things will taint them somehow. Claiming my life means claiming my death; they don't want to touch either. My patients in pediatrics—eight-year-olds in casts and wheelchairs—dream they see me in white rags, bleeding, coming toward them down the hall. They clutch Fran's hands in the dark. Did he know me? they ask. Did he know me well? Fran shakes his head and clears his throat, and after a long while says, No, not really. He does not tell them that he could not identify me at the morgue. He does not tell them that he can no longer remember my face; when he tries to remember my face he sees the photo in the papers, blurred and bland and blond; the face reminds him of his sister, mother, teacher, not me. He releases the small hot hands and walks down the hall. As he passes the new nurse on duty he tells her never to walk out alone. She looks astounded. It would never occur to her to do so. She is not like me. No one is like me.

Except maybe you. You, frowning as you walk faster and faster across the hard sand, you are like me. You, wondering how to shake the shadow of my voice from the perfect day that shines around you—yes, you are a lot like me. And I'm going to keep talking to you, you know. Whether you're on the beach or in bed with a lover or laughing with friends—I'm going to talk to you all your life until you recognize me and know who I am.

The Writers' Model

I'M OLD NOW, BUT when I was young you could talk me into anything. I had an open mind. So when I saw the ad saying some "professional writers" needed an "adventurous girl" to "interview for fictional purposes," I was intrigued, especially when the ad went on to say that "by simply answering questions" I could "make an important contribution to American literature." I had always wanted to make an important contribution to something, so I threw on my coat, grabbed my purse, and went straight to the address listed in the paper.

I found myself outside a dark house in a bad part of town. Nobody answered when I knocked so I tried the door and stepped into the strangest room, like an interrogation cell in a jail, with one bare bulb in the middle of the ceiling and an empty chair waiting beneath it. A ring of silent people circled the chair. I caught the glint of their pens and pencils and saw the notepads open on their laps. All the notepads, I noticed, were blank. For some reason, that touched me. I straightened my shoulders, went to the chair, and sat down.

"Ask me anything," I said, and the first writer said, "What is your body like?"

I stared. I realized that all the people were men and that many were dressed alike, in tweed jackets with leather patches on the sleeves. One by one they adjusted their horn-rimmed glasses, lit their briar pipes, patted the Irish setters lying at their feet, and looked at me as if they expected me to take my clothes off.

So I did. I am not shy and I had already understood that to these writers I was neither woman nor human; I was an object. An *objet* (I comforted myself) *d'art*.

"Why are you smiling?" one writer asked, and I told my little joke as I took my scarf off, and another said, his voice sharp, "Do you know French?" and I shrugged as I unbuttoned my blouse because everyone knows some French and then I stepped out of my skirt and for the rest of that first session there was nothing but scribbling and an occasional testy, "How about German? How about Greek?" from the back.

I didn't have to do many sittings stark naked after that; they had their notes to refer to, after all, and the small room was cold. It wasn't my body they had come for anyway, it was the questions—the questions and the answers I gave them. Many of them had seen a woman, touched a woman, had sex with a woman—many of them were married—but not many had ever really talked to a woman, and this was their chance.

How do you feel about your underpants?

Do you jiggle when you run?

What is it like to have someone inside you?

Does size really matter?

What does orgasm feel like?

Those were the physical questions, some of them, though of course there were many more. Everything about breasts fascinated them except nursing—they did not care to hear about that—and very few asked about menstruation or childbirth. They all wanted to know about "the first time" and if I'd done it with women, or had it done to me as a child. Nymphomania intrigued them and they could not hide their disbelief when I said that neither I nor any of my girlfriends knew anything about it. The other, non-physical, questions were more varied but not really much more surprising:

Do you fish?

Do you dream?

Do you vote?

And, the one that made them all hold their breath:

Do you read?

At the break, many continued to write as they watched me sip my tea from a thermos, eat half my sandwich. They were allowed to smell my perfume and look through my purse. When I went to the toilet it was permitted for one or two to come with me and watch, take notes if they needed.

After the break a few presented me with "problems" they "had blocked" on—those were the words they used. You are about to be stoned for adultery: how do you feel? Your husband has run off with another woman: what do you do? Your brother is kidnapped, your daughter is raped, you are raped, there's a lion charging toward you, there's a corpse in your closet—easy stuff, most of it, nothing, I thought, to get blocked by. Sometimes they brought costumes for me—snake suits or nurse uniforms or frilled gingham aprons, depending on what kind of character they were trying to depict— and they would ask me to act out a fight scene with a lover, or improvise a suicide note, or pose with a whip, or pretend to go crazy—and all that was easy too.

The only part of the job that was not easy was Free Form Time—the five minutes reserved at the end of each session for me to talk about the things that I'd been thinking about during the week. There was a lot I wanted to talk about, everything from school board elections to mermaid sightings to Mexican railroads, but the writers were tired by then, and as cranky as children. Some swallowed yawns, others openly doodled, many just leashed their dogs and left. I saw I was not holding their attention and I had to fight the temptation to start making things up. If I'm not careful, I thought in a panic, I will turn into a writer myself.

Looking back I see it was a good job in many ways. The men were lonely and ignorant, but they were educable, I thought, and I took pride in helping them, however slightly, understand others. When I saw that a few female characters based on me were being called "real" and "rounded" in the book reviews, I was, frankly, flattered. But when I read the books themselves I saw nothing had changed. The women in these books were the same as they'd always been—the same saints, sluts, and sorry set of psychotics that I had been reading about all my life. Where were their passions? Their generous hearts? Where had I failed?

The writers' questions began to tire me—that same one, week after week, about the underpants—and I decided to quit before I became what they saw. With the money I'd saved I finished school and since then I've been a milliner, a chef, a sand castle architect. I've run child care centers and nursing homes. I put up wallpaper one autumn in Australia, worked the vineyards in Brittany, clocked bicycle races in Houston. I've always been drawn to the odd job, in every sense of that phrase, and I wasn't too surprised to see a spaceship land in my backyard last night. The little man who got out looked familiar, with his domed forehead and hard hurt stare. He had come a long way, he said, to study someone like me. And much as I'd like to see Mars, I picked up the shotgun and marched him right off my porch. Some things can't be studied, I told him, and there is no one like me.

The Language Burier

THE IDEA CAME TO MRS. ARDIS as she was showing Mr. Ikado where to plant tulips. It was such a good idea that she left the little gardener on his knees, got into her car, and drove down through the canyon to her son's house at once. At first the cabin looked deserted. But she knew Colette and the baby were there because she could hear Colette singing in that language that was neither quite French, nor quite English, nor quite anything but peculiar. "Sacrazabadieu," Mrs. Ardis mimed. She crossed the clearing, ran up the wooden steps, and made her way through the small, darkened rooms to the back deck. Colette was sitting cross-legged in the sunlight, rocking back and forth with the baby. When she saw Mrs. Ardis she froze for a second, then she started rocking again. "I did not suspect you," she said.

"Expect," Mrs. Ardis corrected. "I did not expect you would expect me." She held out her hands to take the baby. "Come on," she said. She snapped her fingers. "Let her see Grandma." When Colette did not move, Mrs. Ardis sighed and scooped the baby up herself. "You," she whispered to Kiki, "are the spitting image of your daddy, yes you are." For Mark too had had white hair at six months, and fat pleated lips, and the grave concentration of one listening, very hard, to a difficult lesson. Mrs. Ardis touched the tip of her nose to the tip of the child's, breathed deeply, and turned to Colette. "How'd you like to rake in a few fast bucks?" she asked. "I just had a brainstorm. You could make a small killing."

Colette did not take her eyes off the child, but when Mrs. Ardis snapped her fingers again she raised her face.

"Bucks," she said. "They are deers?"

"No dear heart," Mrs. Ardis said, "they are not. Bucks are money. Dollars. Moola." She looked at Colette and sighed. Colette had a flushed, freckled, sullen face, and when she frowned, as she was frowning now, all the light left her eyes, and she looked half-witted, or worse. There were times when Mrs. Ardis wondered what, if anything, the nuns at Saint Esprit had been able to teach her. Perhaps the sisters in that tiny cloister were half-witted too. Or perhaps they couldn't read English. For the ad—Mrs. Ardis clearly remembered writing every word of the ad—was in plain simple English. "Wanted," it read, "experienced au pair girl for California household: must be industrious, good-natured, bright, and bilingual." Two weeks later Mrs. Ardis had received a flowery letter from the abbess in Paris and a month later she had opened her door to Colette: confused, disheveled, unsmiling, and mute.

"Rake?" Colette said now. "I will rake the money?"

"You will make money. You will make a great deal of money if you will just start teaching French to my friends. You know my friends. Lily Willis. Deedee. Maybe Ruthanne. They're dying to learn. And you're so convenient. A foreigner. Family. It will be good for you too, dear heart. You'll find your English will improve too. You'll be killing two birds with one stone."

Colette drew a small silver cross from a chain around her neck and began to finger it. Mrs. Ardis turned and paced the deck with the baby. "It's no skin off my nose," Mrs. Ardis said. She stopped to snap the dead leaves off a geranium plant with her strong nails. "I don't care if you and Mark want to throw your lives away." She glanced around the deck. It was so cluttered with tools and books and bicycle parts that it gave her a headache. Even the shadow patterns of leaves on the boards made a mess. "Why should I care how you live? I should be like Mark's father and write you both off. But I can't. Not with Kiki. She's my only child's only child and she deserves the best in the world. Don't you agree?"

"She is a good one," Colette said, looking up at the baby.

"I knew you'd agree!" cried Mrs. Ardis. "Don't you want to know how much you'll make?" She whispered a sum to Kiki and smiled. "We'll have the lessons out here. I'll get it cleaned up. I'll take care of it all. What do you say?"

Colette said nothing. Mrs. Ardis raised her fingers to snap them again, but Kiki bobbed forward, fastened her lips on Mrs. Ardis's knuckle, and started to suck. Mrs. Ardis drew her hand away at once. She looked at it, then wiped her jade ring dry on her skirt. She watched curiously as Colette exposed a small freckled breast, took the baby, and started to nurse. Then she slapped her hands on her hips and looked around. "You'll be glad you agreed," she said. Colette, head bent, rocked back and forth. "Now my friends will learn French, you'll start a nest egg, and Kiki will get to know her own grandma at last. What could be better?"

A bettor is someone who bets on a horse. A hoarse is a frog you get in your throat. A large frog in a small throat is the spitting image of two birds in the bush killed by one stone, making a small killing which fast bucks flee before their noses get skinned.

Colette raised her head from the notebook and tapped her chin with her pen. Did I leave something out? Was there anything else I forgot to write off?

She looked at the baby and thought.

The dream cloud?

Ah yes. The brainstorm.

Colette wrote the new words down and then looked up at the flicker of sunlight through the laurel leaves. After a minute she began to sing again, starting where she had stopped when Mrs. Ardis walked in. Her song was about the nuns at Saint Esprit and the words that they taught her.

Honor, Colette sang. Mercy. Obedience. Bliss.

The friends had been friends, Lily Willis told Colette, wonderful friends, forever, and this was odd because Lily had grown up in Texas, and Kate Ardis came from Canada, and Deedee was from Seattle, making Ruthanne Canova the only native Californian, the only real Californian, but since settling here, on the coast, it was as if, well, it did seem like forever sometimes. "Of course," she concluded, "we were all Mu La's. Mu Lamda's," she explained, as Colette leaned forward to stare at her lips. "The sorority, you know? So we had something in common, right from the start. I like to think," Lily Willis said, "that we've made a sort of international sisterhood out here." She lifted a fist. Her diamonds flashed in the sun.

"Hurrah," said Ruthanne.

"Rah rah," said Deedee.

Mrs. Ardis clapped her hands and Colette leaned forward, looking into each face. The women were sitting in a circle on the new canvas chairs Mrs.

Ardis had ordered, sipping tea from the cups she had brought, eating cakes from the bakery she had asked to deliver. The day before, Mr. Ikado had swept the deck, repaired the railing, and dragged large redwood planters in from his truck. Colette had shouted in her very best English to please leave at once or she'd call to the sheriff, but Mr. Ikado had never paid any attention to Colette, and he paid none now; he knelt, his back to her, and silently filled the new planters with new plants, already in flower. When Mark came home he found Colette sitting inside, in the dark, with her hands in her lap, rocking.

"What's she done now?" Mark asked. Colette sniffled and shrugged toward the back deck. Mark looked out, saw the chairs and the flowers. "That's not so bad," Mark said. "Once I had a tree house and she climbed up a ladder and wallpapered it." He laughed. Then he sat down and put his arm around his wife. "She'll learn," he said, his lips in Colette's tangled curls. "She'll learn that you're my woman now and not her girl. She can't lay a finger on you anymore."

Colette closed her eyes and saw Mrs. Ardis's finger, short and strong and tiled like a house with one bright red nail. She saw it come crashing down the canyon and through the cabin roof. She closed her eyes tighter. Mark kissed her and laughed again and got up to see the baby. "Say 'Daddy,'" he said, leaning over the crib. "Say 'Dah-dee.'" That night Colette dreamed of the convent gardens, the gnarled wisteria and the cages of larks and rabbits. She could see the old orchard and smell the peaches the sisters threw down from the trees. The next day the first things she saw were the new flowers in the new planters, chrysanthemums and zinnias. They made splashes of brown, bronze, copper, and red against the edge of the forest. Their scent was sharp and dirty and when the wind came they hissed.

"Now," Ruthanne said, sniffing her cup, "what do we call this?"

"Du thé," Colette said. "Tea."

"I made it myself," Mrs. Ardis interrupted. "Because, as you'll recall, Colette's idea of cooking is to throw some bags in a pot and boil them like lobsters. This is made with special herbs from Mr. Ikado's herb plot." She took a sip. "What do you think?"

"Scrumpdiddlyumptious," the women said.

Colette leaned forward.

"Scrumpdiddlyumptious," the women repeated.

Colette pressed her fingers to her lips but the women laughed out loud and Deedee said, "Oh, pain and sorrow girls, when will we grow up," and Lily said, "Not until we have to," and Ruthanne said, "Nothing has changed, we're all still the same," and Colette nodded at that because it was true: they were all the same. They all had short curly hair, cut like petals around their small faces. They all wore denim skirts and cowboy shirts and low-heeled shoes with golf socks. They had thin arms, thin legs, thick waists, deep tans. When Colette first came from France one of them had given her a tennis racket and one had given her a bicycle and one had given her a ski parka with just two tears in the lining. One woman had helped her put away a wash load of party dishes, and one had said, of Mrs. Ardis, "Don't mind her, her heart's in the right place"—a phrase Colette recalled, pondered, and entered into her notebook. For even then she knew that words like *heart* and *place* were going to be complex. Simple words always were. But the women knew nothing of this. They sat and smiled and sipped their tea, and they were as they had always been—generous and kind, just a little silly, perhaps, but very kind, all of a kind, kind of kind.

Colette sang the song of the women to Kiki and when she was through she said, What kind are you?

But Kiki put her fingers in her mouth and shook her head and wouldn't tell.

Then I'll guess, said Colette. And she guessed succotash, mudplop, persimmon, mosquito. And Kiki laughed at every word, and Colette laughed too, because these words were funny and new and utterly useless. After the laughter she began singing again. There were a thousand sounds Kiki must learn, a thousand to echo and offer.

Humility, Colette sang. Devotion. Discipline. Grace.

Mrs. Ardis led her friends along the clearing. "Hear that?" she said. She stopped, her square hand lifted, her jade ring like a shield.

Someone was singing. The women stumbled against each other, blinking in the sunlight. The voice was high and sweet and steady. The women squinted at the cabin, the cornfield in the clearing, the dark blue and heather colors at the forest edge. The melody was like a medieval mass, and the words were unfamiliar—but of course, the women thought, Colette sings in French.

"That's not French," Mrs. Ardis said. "It's not Latin. Or Japanese. Or Eskimo. It's gibberish." She looked at the women. "Nice way for Kiki to learn to talk I don't think."

"Now Kate," soothed Lily, "it's probably some old lullaby."

"A folk tune."

"A ballad."

Mrs. Ardis shook her head. "No," she said. "It's more than that, worse than that, and I don't understand it at all."

"Who could?" Deedee said. "There's a language barrier."

"There's more than that," Mrs. Ardis repeated. "There's a sense of...I don't know...secrets. I don't like secrets," said Mrs. Ardis. "Listen to that."

But the singing had stopped.

"Sometimes I think those nuns in the cloister were witches." Mrs. Ardis smiled briefly, unhappily. "Sometimes I think they taught Colette how to cast spells and curses. Other times I tell myself, Don't be silly, Kate, it's simply that the girl is a raving schizophrenic."

"She's just a young girl," said Ruthanne.

"Who's made Mark very happy," said Lily.

"And given you a grandchild," said Deedee.

But Mrs. Ardis wasn't listening to the women. "I just don't know what to believe," she said at last.

"We should believe the best."

"And get on with our lives."

"Well what on earth do you think we are doing?" Mrs. Ardis snapped.

And the women had to laugh at that because it was true, they were getting on with their lives. They were all playing golf and tennis and backgammon and selling real estate and antique furniture and doing aerobics and Zen meditation and saving whales and sending checks to their children and checks to their parents and taking calcium and training their dogs and cooking without cholesterol for their husbands, and as if that wasn't enough—and perhaps it wasn't enough—they were now walking, single file, across the bright clearing and up the steps and through the dark little house and out to the sun-dappled deck to learn French.

"Pourquoi?" asked Colette.

She poured out the last cup of tea and smiled at the women. The women smiled back. The lesson began. Sunlight flashed over hands, shoulders, feet. A white moth hovered at the stiff, frilled mouth of a chrysanthemum, quivered off, hovered at the mouth of another. *"Pourquoi?"* Colette repeated.

Lily said she was going to France soon, taking a barge trip down the Loire, and she wanted to know how to say: Look! How pretty!

"*C'est beau*," smiled Colette.

Ruthanne said that since she had bought a Cuisinart she thought she'd better at least learn to pronounce the word *cuisinart*. Joe expected French food every night now; he expected her to turn into Julia Child!

"*Bien*," said Colette.

Deedee said she had studied French years ago, as a girl, and when she quit school to get married her professor had said, "Don't go quietly into that dark night"—something like that, funny, not even French, but she never forgot it. So here she was, years later: voilá.

"Voilá," said Colette.

Mrs. Ardis said she was only doing it to keep up with Kiki. It was bad enough that Colette talked in tongues. It wouldn't do, would it, dear heart, to have Kiki start babbling too? "No," Mrs. Ardis said, "I want to understand you, dear heart. I want to understand you both."

Colette poured the cold tea, cup by cup, onto the flower roots. The women were gone, but she still heard their voices. She threw cake crumbs over the railing and into the corn field below. When Kiki awoke she picked her up, rocked back and forth, and sang the song of the dear heart. She held Kiki close as she sang it, so Kiki could feel the quick kick of the hart as it leapt ahead of the hunter. She sang with her cheek on the baby's chest and when she stopped singing she heard a small beat start up and come close, and that is why, Kiki seemed to be saying, there are two of us, deer hart.

The lessons began with short verbs like *come* and *go*, and nouns Colette could point to. At first the women were hesitant but as the weeks went on they gained confidence. They nudged each other, smiled, jostled each other's shoulders and hips; sometimes, in their eagerness, they even accidentally scratched each other with their diamond rings. *La lune! La jupe! Les arbres!* Or, more softly, seriously: *le pain, la pomme, les gâteaux*.

After vocabulary came the grammar drill: *je parle*, I speak; *vous parlez*, you speak. And sometimes Colette praised them and sometimes she tipped her head and twisted her silver cross and rocked back and forth as if they weren't even there, and then the women felt uneasy and glanced at each other while Mrs. Ardis smiled slightly and cleaned the tip of one short red nail with the tip of another. Ruthanne had a trick for such times.

"I think I hear Kiki," Ruthanne would say. "Yes, I'm sure I hear your baby."

Then Colette had no choice but to look up, sniff, rise, and depart. And after she left to see if that slight rustle in the air was, indeed, her baby, the women would laugh a little together, relaxed. Mrs. Ardis, looking up at the trees with that small slight smile, might also say, Wasn't it odd, the way Colette sniffed the air, as if she was one animal and Kiki another, as if people had odors—not that they didn't; even outdoors, Colette had an odor. Most foreigners did, of course. Mr. Ikado, for instance, smelled distinctly of vinegar, but Colette's odor was even more peculiar; she smelled like burnt cloth and rotting leaves. It was one of the first things Mrs. Ardis had noticed about her, working, as they had, side by side in the kitchen. Underneath the onions and cleanser and bacon and thyme: *mon Dieu!* Still smiling, Mrs. Ardis looked at her friends and held her nose.

Kiki, however, was beautiful. Everyone agreed. Kiki made it all worth it. Here came Colette, with Kiki in her arms. What a little doll! What a darling dumpling! Mrs. Ardis snapped her fingers, held out her arms, and set Kiki to ride at once on her knees. Kiki rode like a circus dancer with her back straight and her fingers poised and her short light hair floating up and down. The women watched and Colette watched too, leaning forward, her fingers locked into a net.

"I remember," Mrs. Ardis said, "the first day I met Colette. I took her cold damp little hands in mine and I said, 'So, dear heart, you are my girl from Gaul, my broad from abroad, my au pair from Paree'—and she blinked and flinched, you know how she pulls back, quick, like a little clawed cat— and I thought perhaps she didn't know I was joking so I raised my voice and said it again and there was still no reaction, just this blank look. She didn't understand me. And she didn't want to try." Mrs. Ardis shook her head. Mr. Ikado, at her feet, silently dug up gladiolus corms with a sharp spade and piled them on the lawn. "Soon," Mrs. Ardis continued, "I realized other people couldn't understand me either. I said to Mr. Ardis, 'That girl Colette's a little strange the way she sings all day,' and Mr. Ardis said, 'She sings because she's happy here.' Happy? Clutching that crucifix and cowering under the cupboards? I said to Mark, 'Stay away from that French girl, there's something wrong with her head, she should go see a doctor,' and Mark said, 'Don't you love her hair, the way it curls? Doesn't she have lovely eyes?' Nobody understood me," Mrs. Ardis said. "It was very peculiar." She picked up one of the long yellow roots and began flicking the tiny seedlike cormels off it with her strong red nails. "It was like talking to you," she said, as Mr. Ikado dug down with his spade. "It was like talking Japanese to someone stone deaf."

Mr. Ikado looked up, and, startled to see her there, standing so close, smiled a bright merry smile, his teeth as small and golden as the seeds.

One night in November the chrysanthemums turned to brown sticks, no one knew why; it happened like that, snap! It must have been frost though there hadn't been frost. The zinnias bloomed a week longer, then they too died. Mr. Ikado came and carted them off in his truck. Colette watched from the window. Leaves fell. Broad brown leaves from the madrone trees, slim yellow speckled leaves of laurel. The afternoons were still warm and the women still sat outside with their notebooks and their tea and they were still having fun, such a good time, they hadn't laughed so hard in years. There were afternoons when they could barely make it through the vocabulary and the grammar drills and sometimes there were little poems and sometimes funny riddles and honestly they were out of breath from laughing and they felt as lightheaded as girls, giddy, and Colette laughed with them, flashing deep, surprising dimples, her silver cross leaping up and down on the pulse at her throat, and Mrs. Ardis laughed too as she bounced the baby on her long, hard thighs, and it was all very good and gave them only the slightest headache, after, from laughing—but their skills were improving, they were getting much better, *trop mieux* (or something like that), more sure of themselves anyway. So when Colette began telling the stories, they could almost understand what she was saying. There was a story about a farmer who sold his daughter, and a story about nuns climbing trees in a garden, and a story about a queen with a magic tongue who turned words into birds and caged them.

"Now you," Colette said to Deedee, "you must try to tell us a story, in French."

Deedee said, "Oh, no, I can't," and flushed, and then, in French, said, "Long ago there was a young girl. She loved a professor. But he was married. So she married someone else. The end."

Colette touched Deedee's hand, corrected five words, and turned to Ruthanne. "Will you say a story? In French?"

Ruthanne licked her lips and said, "Today is my husband Joe's birthday. He is fifty-eight years old. I have made him a cake with the Cuisinart. I hope he chokes."

Colette blinked, corrected Ruthanne's pronunciation, and turned to Lily. Lily clasped her hands, looked off toward the trees, and said, "Look how pretty it is here. The sky is so pretty and the trees are so pretty and you are very pretty too, Colette."

Colette sat back, pleased with the women.

"What about Grandma?" Mrs. Ardis drawled. She sat outside the circle, with Kiki on her lap. She had slipped the jade ring off her finger and given it to Kiki to play with. Kiki turned the big stone around and around. "Doesn't anyone want to hear Grandma's story?"

"But of course," said Colette.

"But of course," mimed Mrs. Ardis. There was a pause. Then she threw back her head and began to speak and the words that poured out were in such perfect, rapid, impassioned French that her three friends set their tea cups in their saucers and their saucers on their knees and stared at her. Only Colette did not look surprised. Colette sat very straight and still with her head tipped, her eyes closed.

"One day," Mrs. Ardis began, "a strange girl came to work in my kitchen. She was sullen and secretive, dirty and slow. She couldn't cook. She couldn't clean. She sang nonsense all day as she worked. This was bad enough. But it wasn't the worst. The worst was when she began to steal."

The women looked at each other. "You'll have to slow down," Ruthanne said. "We can't understand you."

Mrs. Ardis looked at Colette. "Can you understand me?"

Colette nodded. Kiki laughed and pressed the cold jade to her lips.

"First she stole my voice," said Mrs. Ardis. "I would open my mouth to tell her something and she would pluck the words out of the air, one by one, and drop them into her apron pocket. Then she would look at me with those big blank eyes, all innocence, and do exactly what she pleased. Next my face disappeared. I would have it on when I went into the kitchen but her dullest glance could pare it off and toss it aside and when I patted my face it felt featureless as an old potato. Next to go were my husband's eyes. He had to squint when he looked at me. He began to blink and purse his lips over his pipe as if he had never seen me before. I said, 'Do I look like an old potato to you too?' and he said, 'No. You look like a spoiled, idle, rude woman to me, and I don't like to look at you much anymore.' Finally," Mrs. Ardis said, "the girl stole my son. First he disappeared from his room at night, then from his college classes by day. She took him from me completely at last and dragged him down here, to this hole in the woods. She left me with nothing."

"That is not true," said Colette.

"No," Mrs. Ardis agreed. "It isn't. She did leave me Kiki."

Colette opened her eyes.

"She did leave me Kiki to keep and care for and raise as my own."

Colette held out her arms. Mrs. Ardis tightened hers. Colette snapped her fingers. Mrs. Ardis laughed.

"Don't you know what happens to thieves?," Mrs. Ardis asked. "They get caught. Especially girl thieves who hear voices and see things—they always get caught. They don't go to jail—not in this day and age—but sometimes they go to nice public hospitals. Sometimes they stay there for years. They rock back and forth, they sing to themselves. It's like a cloister there, in a way. No husbands allowed, of course. No children permitted. These girls are known as incompetent mothers."

"God help you," Colette said.

Kiki said something too. Neither Colette nor Mrs. Ardis heard a word, but the three women heard and looked and saw Kiki's face grow as green and stony as the jade she'd just swallowed. Lily leapt to her feet and lifted Kiki high and Deedee struck her in the small of the back with a sharp rapid fist while Ruthanne knelt and pressed the heel of her hand against the baby's diaphragm. The three women worked like this, in silence, until Kiki coughed and spat the ring out. Mrs. Ardis watched the ring shoot over the railing and land like a grasshopper in the stubble of the cornfield below. Colette only watched the darkness fade from Kiki's cheeks and then she stood, bowed her head over the women's hands, and carried the baby into the house. Mrs. Ardis looked up with her slight, bright smile.

"Quite a show," Mrs. Ardis said. "You must tell me where you learned to do that."

But the women were unhappy and restless and eager to leave; they had no time to explain about their CPR class right now; they had dinners to cook and gardens to water and husbands to meet at the depot. Besides, they were "Frankly upset," as Lily put it, "to find out that Kate knew French the whole time." "It was deceitful of her," Deedee agreed. "We felt we'd been made fools of," Ruthanne summed up. "We felt we'd been used, and we didn't like it a bit."

So the women left the lesson together, trudging across the clearing toward their cars, rattling their car keys in the silence of the canyon. And Mrs. Ardis said she would follow in a minute, but she didn't. She sat on, listening, until the sun went down, and she was still there, listening, when Colette began to sing inside the cabin. She leaned forward, hoping to learn something new, but Colette's words were the same old words, mad and monotonous. She repeated the sounds, but they still made no sense. Later, when Mark came home, Mrs. Ardis leaned forward again. But Mark's words made no sense either, and even his voice—deep, complacent, commanding—was foreign to her. When the moon rose, Mrs. Ardis rose too. She paused for a moment in the shadows outside the lit window. She wished someone would invite her in, and clasp her hand, and look happy to see her. She thought, for no reason, of Mr. Ikado. Mr. Ikado, she thought, would be happy to see her. She went down the back stairs, stooped in the cornfield, retrieved her ring, and slipped it on. As she started her car the cabin door opened a crack and rock music poured out.

She winced and drove off.

Long after she left, long after Mark and Colette had finished playing their music, and turned the sound down, and kissed, and gone to bed; long after the full moon lit the bare boards of the deck, hovered at the forest edge, and sank; long after all that, Kiki woke up. It was dark. She opened her eyes to the dark, then she opened her lips to the dark. She took a small breath. She started to speak.

Cruise Control

"I'M GOING TO MISS YOU, MOM," Kim says. "Really." It is the fourth time she has said it this morning and her voice has taken on a quick, practiced melancholy.

Barbara, who has been going through her purse to see if she has enough money to buy them both breakfast, says, "Me too," with a smile she hopes hides her impatience. She picks a MasterCard charge card out of her wallet and slides it onto the table. "Larry was saying just last night how different it will be, with you gone."

Kim nods, leans her chin on her hand, and looks out the window.

The restaurant is decorated to resemble a country cottage. It is large and dim, hung with chintz curtains and baskets of plastic nasturtiums. A cutout of an aproned woman juggling pancakes hangs from the ceiling. Except for a few warehouse workers and retail clerks, it is empty. Barbara looks with longing at a newspaper being read by a man across the room, then checks her wristwatch once more. The car rental office won't open until nine. That leaves almost an hour before Kim can pick up the car she's reserved. Once they have the car, the day can proceed as planned: Kim will drive back to the house and Barbara will follow. Together they will pack the car with the things Kim needs for college. The teddy bear Kim has had since she was six is waiting on the porch at home, already dressed for the trip in a sun hat and long chiffon scarf. The two younger children and Juanita, the live-in, will present Kim with the bag lunch they've packed. Then everyone will kiss and cry and wave, and Kim will drive to the corner, honk once, and vanish. She will have the map Barbara has marked on the seat beside her, the thin red line drawn up Interstate 80 to Nevada; she will have the guidebooks Barbara has bought and a list of numbers to call in case of emergency—but she will be alone, on her own, for the first time in her life.

"I feel like I'm never going to see you again," Kim says. Her voice is tearful but her face is calm. "I feel like this is our last day together."

"Nonsense," Barbara says. "You'll be home before you know it. You're going to come home for Thanksgiving; you promised."

"Our last day together," Kim repeats, "and I've made you late for work."

Barbara cannot be gracious and say, That's all right. It isn't all right. She works in Larry's downtown office, and today she has to juggle several patient appointments and see the accountant. "It can't be helped," she says, and adds, in an attempt to sound more cheerful, "We haven't been out together in ages. We used to save for weeks, remember, to come to places like this."

"Before you married Larry."

"That's right. Years ago. So this is fun."

"Old times," Kim agrees, in her sad, rapid voice.

"Cheer up," Barbara says. The minute she says it, Kim's eyes fill with tears. Barbara looks down, rubs her thumb on her knife. Sometimes Kim looks exactly like Eric. She has Eric's soft lower lip and graceful, almost helpless looking hands, and she has Eric's trick—but of course it's more than a trick—of making Barbara feel she is in the wrong. Again and again Barbara feels she is dealing with her first husband once more, repeating past failures. She straightens her knife, sighs, and looks up.

"You've been wanting to leave home," she points out, "ever since you were thirteen."

"I know. It's just that now it's here."

"You should be excited."

Kim nods, pulls a Marlboro from her ragged leather purse, lights it with a brisk efficient swipe of her match, inhales gustily, and then slumps, her shoulder following her arm down the length of the table. Barbara wonders if Kim is well enough to drive at all. Her face, in the light from the window, looks tired, patched with dabs of thick makeup. She is wearing a new lipstick in a bright pink shade that's already caked. Her black T-shirt is frayed under the armpits, and she is not wearing a bra. Barbara tucks her own silk blouse into the waistband of her linen skirt and moves to one side as the waitress pours coffee. She is almost twenty, Barbara reminds herself. When I was twenty, I was already her mother. I was married to Eric, going to night school, working two day jobs. "Do you take MasterCard?" she asks the waitress.

"Can we have more cream?" Kim asks at the same time.

The waitress nods to both and returns with a cream pitcher that Kim empties at once into her cup. Barbara picks up a menu and watches as Kim reaches for the sugar. She tries to pull her eyes away from the torn paper packets Kim drops by her saucer.

"Your teeth," she says weakly.

"They're paid for," grins Kim.

"Just barely. Larry sent the final installment last week."

"That Larry of yours," Kim says, licking her coffee spoon, "is a very weird man. You know he didn't even say good-bye to me this morning? I went up to hug him and he put his wallet over his chest, like this, and then he gave me a hundred dollar bill."

Kim opens her purse and shows Barbara the money, lying crumbled in a jumble of cigarette papers, makeup, and loose change. Something else is in the bottom of the purse as well: a diaphragm case. Barbara recognizes the round plastic compact, the same color as her own. She has seen Kim's diaphragm case in many places over the past five years—in her top drawer, in her backpack, on the shelf under the bathroom sink—but she has never had it presented to her as boldly as this. Does she expect to meet someone today? On the road? Barbara looks into Kim's waiting wet eyes.

"I hope you thanked Larry," she says, her voice cold.

"Of course I thanked him. What do you think I am?"

"Ladies? Ready to order?"

"Just an English muffin," Barbara says.

"I wanted a muffin too."

"Well have one."

But Kim shakes her head and orders French toast. "I bet she has a college degree," she says, when the waitress has left. "I bet she has a master's. Remember Carmen, at Guido's? She had her master's."

Guido's? Barbara thinks. Kim has worked in a dozen different places this summer alone. She has been a dog-sitter, housecleaner, file clerk, telephone solicitor, janitor...She has never held a job for more than three weeks and she has not saved a cent.

"The gelato store," Kim prompts.

"Oh. Right. Where you met Abdul."

"They were going to make me the assistant manager," Kim says. "Did I tell you?"

"No." Barbara is puzzled. "Why didn't you stay there?"

Kim shrugs and then laughs, a short laugh that collapses into a low thick cough. I should have had her tonsils taken out, Barbara thinks. I should have made her stop smoking the first time I caught her with a cigarette in her hand.

"I can't get over Larry," Kim coughs. She clutches an imaginary wallet to her heart. "I mean he's an eye doctor for God's sake and he never looks anyone in the eye."

He looks me in the eye, Barbara thinks. He looks our two sons in the eye. She runs her fingertip over the embossed numbers on the credit card. Larry's indifference to Kim has always troubled her, but she has never known how to resolve it. By the time the two met, Kim was already eleven; she was overweight and outspoken and her skin had started to break out. She called Larry "Dr. Butler" six months into the marriage and kissed him goodnight on the mouth. "Where did she come from?" Larry would ask, his face turned aside. And Barbara, answering lightly, "From me," would wonder why Larry— the kindest and most generous man she had ever met—could not see anything good in Kim. You can't make someone love someone else, Barbara reasons. You can't force opposites together.

"I just think you ought to be more grateful to him," she says.

They both reach for their coffee. Kim sips noisily, as if someone were holding her head to the cup. Barbara tries not to let it bother her. There have been times this last year when the simple sound of Kim going sip-sip-sip has made her want to kill her. Other things, just as small, have been as infuriating: uncapped bottles of nail polish, water glasses filled to the brim with white wine, cigarettes stubbed out in the planter box, the teddy bear dressed in the cashmere sweater set Barbara bought Kim for her birthday. The lost and missing items, from the household keys to the new gym shoes to a car—how could Kim have "lost" the car Larry bought her when she agreed to go back to continuation high? Barbara has had the details explained again and again: the friend who borrowed the car and left it unlocked, the subsequent theft, the ultimate crack-up—but Barbara just hears the single word *lost*.

"It seems the only two sentences I ever say at home," Kim says, "are 'Thank you' and 'I'm sorry.' I can't wait to practice the rest of the English language at school. I'm going to study very hard, you know." She puts her coffee cup down, lifts her tired face, and speaks like a hypnotist's subject repeating instructions. "I am going to get all A's and when I graduate I am going to travel for a year and then I will go back and get a graduate degree in clinical psychology and work with children."

"Yes," says Barbara.

"I'd rather sit on the couch and watch old *Lucy* reruns and eat toast all day."

"No," says Barbara.

The waitress sets their plates before them. Kim stubs out the cigarette she has just lit and picks up her fork. Barbara shudders at the careless slosh of syrup over fried bread, then devotes herself to scraping off some of the butter that has pooled into the craters of her own English muffin.

"Last night," Kim says, her mouth full, "I lay awake thinking about all the places we've ever lived in. Wasn't there a big yellow house? In Portland or somewhere?"

"We didn't have the whole house," Barbara corrects. "Just the downstairs."

"With a big street in front? Because that's what I was remembering. I was remembering the time you got so mad at me you told me to go outside. So I went into the street and when you found me you beat me because I wasn't in my room."

Kim has a need to repeat this story—Barbara has heard it a hundred times. She has never known what response Kim expects. She wipes her fingertips on her napkin.

"I don't think I *beat* you," she says. "I spanked you, I suppose." She pauses. "That was just before the divorce." She remembers Kim that year in Portland, trying to teach herself to jump rope on the sidewalk while her parents argued inside a locked kitchen. How odd, Barbara thinks, that she's asked so few questions about Eric and me and that whole early time. She must know we had to get married. But what does she know about the marriage itself? Does she remember how poor we were and how often we had to move? Does she remember Eric standing in tears in the doorway, shaking with a hangover, shouting that everything that had gone wrong in his entire life was my fault and her fault? Everything. Our fault.

"Did you love him?" Kim asks.

Eric has married twice since the divorce and Barbara, startled by Kim's question, cannot ever remember loving him, exactly; no. But she can remember the touch of his soft young lips and the banana-like taste of his skin and she can remember these things as vividly after fourteen years as she can remember making love to Larry last night. "I..." she begins, but Kim interrupts.

"You were too young," Kim decides. "I don't know how you did it. If I had to have a husband and a baby right now..." She shakes her head, her eyes on the huge cardboard woman with her flying pancakes.

Barbara remembers the diaphragm in the bottom of Kim's purse and says briefly, "You're smarter than I was."

"I'll probably never get married anyway. Who would ask me?"

"Lots of men will ask you. You'll meet lots of men this year. This is going to be the best year of your life."

"It will be the best year of your life too," Kim points out. "Having me gone. You and Larry can have your own little family all to yourselves." There is no bitterness in Kim's voice, and Barbara, on guard, says, "It will be good to have the shampoo to myself, yes. And the telephone."

"That reminds me. Did Sean call while I was out last night?"

"Sean?"

"You know."

Barbara does not know. Sean may or may not be one of the well-dressed, perfectly mannered boys in Kim's circle of friends. He may or may not be gay. James and Troy, Kim has said, are lovers. Troy's twin brother, Terry, is an alcoholic. Terry's girlfriend, Lisa, is a heroin addict. Allison is anorexic; Jessica is bulimic. Gordon is out on bail after an attempted burglary of the men's store he clerks for, and Vanessa tried to kill herself by jumping off a friend's speedboat when the band she was singing with fired her. Henry is the friend who left Kim's car unlocked and Henry joined the Navy last month. Or was it the Coast Guard? Barbara has the names and histories but she doesn't have them right. She doesn't try, Kim says. Barbara hears Kim on the phone late at night, the low hesitant questions, the pauses, the excited rush of advice at the end. She is playing therapist already, Barbara thinks. She wonders if Kim will really take her degree in psychology, as she's said. She tries to imagine Kim at forty, cheerful and blowsy, counseling adolescents about their depression.

"No one called then?" Kim says. "Not even Abdul?"

"You're kidding." Barbara puts down her napkin. "You're not still seeing Abdul?"

Kim colors slightly and looks away.

"I thought he went back to his wife. Didn't he go back to his wife?"

"I don't know, Mom."

"Yes or no."

"I don't know," Kim repeats. "I don't pry into my friends' private business."

- 47 -

"Well aren't you the perfect little lady at last."

"If you're going to be hostile..."

"You bet I'm hostile. You promised Larry and me you would stop seeing Abdul six weeks ago."

"You don't like him because he's black."

"That's not true and you know it. I don't like him because he's married. I don't like him because he's thirty years old. That's why I don't like him. Why do you like him?"

"Can we change the subject, please?"

"To what, Kim?"

Kim shrugs. Her face is starting to bubble up. In a second she will be crying and blubbering, her mascara smearing, her earrings jingling, and Barbara will be sitting across from her, back straight, chin up, lips thin, looking as if she hadn't caused it all—looking as if it weren't all her fault. She unclenches her fist in her lap and sighs. If she's going to be bad, Barbara thinks, why doesn't she learn to be bad better? If she's going to sneak off to see Abdul, why can't she just do it, and not ask me if he's called? Can't she learn to conceal her own crimes? She remembers herself, years ago, walking down the aisle in a white dress and two girdles that she hoped hid her shame—for it was shame she felt, then and later, when Eric, in tears, slammed the last door behind him—shame and guilt and fury. "I don't know how you live the way you do," she says, her voice even.

"That's really none of your business, is it."

"Not anymore. No."

"I'm sorry," Kim cries. It's the cry Barbara's been dreading, a high shrill whinny that startles the waitress and makes people along the length of the restaurant look up. Swiftly Barbara slips out of her booth, corners the table, and sits down beside Kim. She puts her arm around Kim's shoulder and presses Kim's head to her neck. "I love you so much," Kim sobs.

"Shhhh," Barbara whispers. She smells her own perfume—Kim must have used it again this morning—and thinks with apprehension of Kim's thick pink lipstick mouthing so close to the heart of her blouse. A man at the counter turns to stare. What do we look like? Barbara thinks, and in the next second, Why should I care? If my daughter wants to bawl her head off in public she can. She glares at the man and hugs Kim hard. "I love you too," she says.

"More than Larry?" Kim asks. Barbara catches her breath—what a coarse, childish question! Kim seems to be holding her breath too. I'll tell her the truth, Barbara thinks. I'll tell her I didn't love Larry, at first. I married him hoping he'd shelter us both. I married him hoping he'd save us. And he did. One of us. She opens her mouth, but Kim, in one of her quick mood changes, laughs. "You should see that old guy at the counter," Kim laughs. "He thinks we're a couple of dykes."

"Oh." Despite herself, Barbara drops her arm. "I hope not," she says. She picks up the check and re-adds the total quickly in her head. "Larry's treat," she says, signing the charge slip.

The sun on the concrete outside is so bright that both Barbara and Kim grope for dark glasses as they walk down the block toward the car rental office. Barbara watches their reflections rise in the plate glass door as they climb the stairs. She can see why the man in the restaurant might not have known they were mother and daughter; she is so dark and angular and Kim is so short and curvy. Kim, seeing the reflection too, stops and whistles. She adjusts the rhinestone frame of her glasses and tugs at the hem of her stained purple shorts. "Wow," she says, "I really look like I belong in Nevada, don't I? Can't you just see me turning into a little old lady who does nothing but play slot machines all day?"

"No," Barbara says warningly. Why Nevada? she wonders again. Kim has told her about the beautiful campus, the excellent psychology department, but Barbara hasn't been able to get the two words *party school* out of her mind. She steps into the office. It reminds her of places she worked in before she met Larry. It has the same slanted venetian blinds, eroded linoleum flooring, scratched blond furniture. The girl behind the desk looks up, already tired at nine in the morning. Perhaps she has a child to raise, Barbara thinks—a daughter she sent off to school with exact change for the bus, a key around her neck, and a telephone number sewn to her jacket.

"Gold car last row," the girl says. She writes up the charge and hands Barbara the keys.

"Gold," Kim whispers, as they step outside. "Did you hear that? Gold." She pries the keys from Barbara's palm and walks quickly through the rows of parked cars. She disappears into the last aisle and Barbara hears her whistle. There, waiting, is a brassy colored sports car with wire wheels and racing stripes.

"You must be kidding," Barbara says.

"You told me to call ahead and get the best deal I could and this is the best deal they had because they need it returned to Reno tonight."

"Don't shout, Kim."

"It's the cheapest car in the lot."

"All right. I believe you."

"I thought you'd be proud of me."

"I am," Barbara says. "I'm impressed."

"Isn't it gorgeous?" Kim unlocks the door with a flourish and flings herself behind the wheel. "Isn't it the most gorgeous car you've ever seen?" The inside of the car is beige plush, like a ring box. Barbara leans in through the window and peers at the dashboard. It might belong on a rocket. "It's just like Eddie Hanken's car," Kim says. "I used to drive Eddie home from concerts all the time. 'It's got five-speed: good. And cruise control.'"

"What's cruise control?" Barbara asks. She is trying to remember who Eddie Hanken is: the boy with the single skull earring or the boy who used to beg from strangers downtown?

"You know. It's on your car. You just never use it. It's a sort of automatic pilot thing where the car drives itself."

"Drives itself?" Barbara does not like the sound of that at all. She has an image of Kim hurtling across the Nevada desert slumped asleep behind the wheel. "Who would want a car that drives itself?"

But Kim isn't listening. "I'll put my teddy bear there," Kim is saying, "and my gardenia plant can go on the floor, and the wind chimes can hang from the mirror."

Barbara straightens and pats the roof of the car. At least it's a small car, she thinks. There's no room for all of Kim's things and a hitchhiker too. She won't get raped; she won't get murdered. "I'll see you back at the house then," she says.

Kim leans out the window. "Hey Mom. Tell me the truth. Do I look good enough to drive this car?"

Barbara stares into Kim's flushed face. Good enough? No, she wants to say, you don't. You don't look good enough or smart enough or old enough to drive any car. You better stay home, where you're safe. With your mother. She opens her mouth then closes it. Luckily, Kim is not looking at her; she is adjusting her reflection in the side view mirror.

"Sean won't believe this," Kim says.

"You're not going to Sean's house," Barbara protests, but Kim has started the car and rock music blares over the roar of the engine. "You're going straight home," Barbara says. Kim gives her a rapt, remote smile as she backs away. She has brushed out her hair and reapplied the pink lipstick. She glows. Barbara watches helplessly as Kim heads out for the freeway. Then she walks back to her own car, the solid grey station wagon that Larry gave her as a wedding gift eight years ago. Her diamond rings glint against the chrome as she unlocks the door. She gets in, adjusts her seat belt, drives to the parking lot exit, and stops. How quiet it is. Not a car on the street. The heat and the silence remind her of something—that morning in Portland when Kim disappeared. She remembers racing through the dark rooms of that downstairs flat, opening closets, groping under couches; she remembers bursting at last into the broad, sunlit street, a wild woman, half-dressed, late for work, clutching an empty wallet and a child's plastic lunch box, her breath thin with panic as she called and called and called again. People had come to their windows to stare. One old man had leaned down from his porch. "Don't worry," he'd said, "your little girlie will find her way home." But by then Barbara could scarcely find her own way home, she was so stunned by the emptiness of the world, and the vast unending way it expanded. Lost, she had thought. Kim's lost, and it's my fault.

She grips the steering wheel and lifts her chin. It all worked out, she tells herself. It all worked out just fine. She looks to the right. She looks to the left. No one is coming. She can go.

Smoke and Mirrors

I LIKED HIM BUT I couldn't tell if he liked me. His wife said he did. She said I cheered him up. Even then people were calling him "poor." Poor Pierre: he worked so hard and had so little to show for it. He left for the print shop at five every morning, his wife said, and came home late, too tired to eat, too tired to talk to her or play with her children, too tired, she said, her voice rising so everyone could hear it, to make love.

This was said at a dinner party. We all looked at our plates, embarrassed. One of the engineers praised the wine; the basketball coach asked for more bread. The ex-gymnast said she hardly met anyone anymore who truly enjoyed his or her job. Pierre, beside me, kept right on eating. He had finished his salad and had started on mine. The little white cat he had found down at the print shop sat on his lap.

"His what?" Suzanne said. "His job?" Her hot tearful gaze moved from the gymnast to Pierre to me. "Are we talking about his goddamn job?" She was already quite drunk. Someone, the coach or my husband, Carter, had taken a flower from the centerpiece and poked it into the front of her half-opened dress, for modesty's sake. She swayed as she stared at us and the bracelets on her wrists fell back with a clatter as she touched her fingertips to her heart.

"*You* know what's wrong with Pierre," she said to me, her voice breaking. "You understand him, don't you?"

"No," I said.

"Suzanne?" Someone was always trying to soothe her. "Would you shut up? Just eat your dinner. It's delicious."

"I can't," Suzanne said. "You'll have to feed me." She closed her eyes and opened her mouth while the first engineer tied a napkin around her throat and the second engineer put a slice of avocado between her bright orange lips.

Carter glanced at his watch. "It's eleven already," he said to no one, "and we're still on the salad." He gave me a pitiful look; I shrugged. *He* was the one who had wanted to come; Suzanne was *his* cousin. I tugged my short black skirt over my knees and moved my foot away from Pierre's.

"How do you stand it?" I asked.

Pierre didn't answer. I listened to the steady click of his knife and fork and his loud rough breath as he swallowed and chewed. I was used to Pierre's sounds by now, although the first time Suzanne had sat me next to him I had been so appalled I had put down my own knife and fork and stared. He ate like an animal and he was always in motion: pleating his napkin, tapping his silver, tugging at the caned underside of my chair or his. His right foot tapped constantly and sometimes his whole body, for no reason, shuddered. It was disturbing and exciting, I decided at last, to have someone so alive and locked up sit so close. He shook his hair back and glared at me. His braces—he was the only adult I had ever known who wore braces—glittered in the candlelight. I couldn't tell if he was upset by Suzanne's theatrics or so used to them he no longer paid attention. I couldn't tell much with Pierre. "So," he said, in his high gentle voice, "what's new?"

I smiled, uncertain; it seemed to be a standing joke between us that nothing was new with me or ever would be. I had a quiet life with Carter. We had been married four years. We did not have children—Carter didn't want them; he had been a bachelor for a long time before he met me and had the habits of a bachelor still. I worked downtown in his office a few mornings a week and did volunteer work at the hospital in the afternoons. Lately I had been thinking about going back to college, to get my degree, although what I would do with it, I didn't know. I was twenty-five and couldn't yet see myself "out there," as Carter called it, "in the real world."

"I finished those curtains I was making," I told Pierre. "I had a lot of trouble with the double pleats but I figured it out." I waited for him to laugh with me at this, but Pierre shot me a soft look of pleasure; he liked to hear about domestic accomplishments, I remembered, and had once introduced me to another guest as "the last of the homemakers." Suzanne, I knew, was no homemaker. She had beautiful things from her earlier marriages, but everything in her old two-story house was in disrepair: there were huge rips in the Persian carpets, a hole punched out of the Tiffany lampshade, cigarette burns on the French pine dining table where we all sat.

"Still reading?" Pierre asked.

The question startled me. Was it a joke? "I'm always reading," I explained. He seemed to be waiting. "Right now I'm reading this poet. Rimbaud. You'd like him. He's...dark."

"Dark?"

I laughed and tugged again at my skirt, looking down at my polished nails, inhaling my own perfume. I had taken an hour to dress for this party; Carter had whistled when he'd seen me step out in my heels and black lace. "He's even darker than you are," I said. Pierre's long hand sidled up the back of my chair, touched my bare neck, pinched it, pulled back, dropped to pet the small white cat still curled on his lap. The others had started to chatter again around us, and Suzanne was laughing at the far end of the table. No one saw me blush or would know, if they did, that I had just betrayed the small book of poems that lay face down on my sewing table at home. I had used Rimbaud, and my excited solitary reading of him the night before, in the same way I had used Grieg once, and Edward Hopper once before that— I had used him as a way of getting Pierre to notice me and see a sister soul.

I don't know why I thought he would. Pierre didn't read books—Suzanne had told us that—he didn't even read newspapers. He had never finished high school. Yet he seemed to feel things; he trembled on beat when the basketball coach played his banjo after dinner, and his hand passing the blue cloisonné bowl the ex-gymnast had brought back from China trembled too as he showed me the design he saw there, a flurry of peonies and butterflies I would not have seen on my own. Secretly I thought Pierre looked like an artist: he was slim and round-shouldered, with long fingers and fine red hair that curled down on his neck. He dressed like an artist, too, in black turtlenecks and soft black jeans. He had a cache of odd knowledge and eccentric skills, and the life he'd led before he met Suzanne, moving from job to job and state to state in a battered pickup truck, with nothing for company but a marijuana plant named Joe, fascinated and inflamed me. What courage it must have taken, I thought, to live outside convention like that! How I wished I had the daring, someday, to take off on my own. I followed Pierre's fork as it trembled in the air like a divining rod and pointed down at my plate.

"You have a visitor," he said.

I looked down and saw, amid the lettuce leaves, nasturtium buds, and one long strand of Suzanne's dyed hair, a small brown snail. Pierre picked it up by the shell. "Hello, Mr. Snail," he said. "Shall we go back to the garden?"

Suzanne turned as he left, her eyes watchful in their smudged tangle of lashes. She was still, despite the weight she had gained and the rosy rash drinking had started to give to her face, the glamorous girl cousin that Carter had always looked up to. Her earrings rattled as she turned to the basketball coach and touched his hand. "He's a genius," she said, of the departing Pierre. "Look. He made this." She pulled a locket from between her breasts and held it out. It was a strange locket, I thought, but I was not thinking clearly. I longed to have been invited into the garden with Mr. Snail; I burned to crouch in the dark with Pierre, away from the others. The locket, I saw, was made of some dull grey metal, formed in the shape of a tear, instead of a heart. "He made it from scraps he found down at the shop," Suzanne said. Her voice began to grow fierce again. The ex-gymnast asked, "Oh, does it have a picture?" and Suzanne nodded and opened the locket and we all saw a little mirror inside.

"Interesting," Carter said. He winked at me; I knew what he thought of Pierre's handiwork. He had been asked to praise other things Pierre had made: a black baby sweater he had knit Suzanne's godchild, a stringed musical instrument he had invented that only played four notes, a walking stick he had carved with a donkey's head for Suzanne, when she fell down the stairs after one of her parties and twisted her foot.

"I think it's beautiful," I said loudly. Both engineers chimed in and we all looked away as Suzanne, on cue, began to cry. "Oh," she cried, "I should never have married him."

That, I thought, was true. Why had she married him? She was ten years older than Pierre; she'd been married three times before. "I thought I could change him," she said, wiping her eyes. "I must have been crazy. Don't ever," she said this to me, for she had decided, at our first meeting, that I was unworldly and needed instruction on life and men, "ever try to change anyone but yourself. It doesn't work. It never works."

I nodded, glum, and rose to clear the table. The engineers had told me how Suzanne had tricked Pierre into marriage—how she'd picked him up at a street fair, brought him home to work on her house, arranged to have her last husband—a tax lawyer—find the two of them in bed. "It was chivalrous of Pierre to take any responsibility at all," one of the engineers had said, and the other had added: "He could have run. Instead he agreed to pay all her debts and help fight the custody suit." I openly marveled at Pierre's generosity, but Carter was less impressed. "That guy knew what the deal was," he said, in defense of Suzanne. "He'd still be living in a truck if it weren't for her. Suzanne may be a little...relaxed...in her lifestyle, but she's got a good heart."

I looked at Carter as I cleared the plates. Carter too, I knew, had a good heart. But I used to think he had more. I used to think he hid his insights and wisdom and creativity on purpose, as protection. It had been hard to accept that Carter hid nothing; he was exactly what he always said he was: an easygoing junior executive who liked sports and making money. Not the savior-prince I'd imagined when we first met, but whose fault was that? Carter hadn't changed. I just hadn't imagined him correctly.

"I know it's my fault," Suzanne was saying. "I give too much. But I can't help it. That's the way I am." I mimed her voice in my head as I carried plates to the kitchen. I had heard Carter's mother and sister say the same exact words.

I liked Suzanne's kitchen far more than I liked Suzanne; it was big and cluttered, full of copper cooking pots and bright with children's drawings and flowering plants and her own long loopy yarn weavings hanging from twigs on the walls. I bent to spoon some scraps into the white cat's dish and patted its bony back. The fur was sleek and oily; it was still half-wild and its purr was as rough as Pierre's own breath. I opened the back door to let it out as two of Suzanne's children pounded down the stairs and helped themselves to a bottle of wine. There were five children in all: three fat, freckled, pale-eyed boys and two thin, dark Vietnamese orphans. They spoke only to each other, never to adults. I watched them slip back up the stairs, then I closed the back door. The garden was dark, no sign of Pierre. He might have left. He often did. Sometimes he'd just disappear and sit up on the roof—Suzanne told us this—or he'd wheel one of her children's bikes off the porch and pedal through the city streets toward the ocean. I finished rinsing the dishes and started back to the party, but stopped in the hall when I saw Pierre. He was standing with his back to me, reading the titles of the books on the bookshelf. How had he come in? Why hadn't I seen him? I felt my heart lift inside me; he was so odd, so original; he gave me a feeling I had never had before, of hushed and violent hilarity. I wanted to roar with laughter and I wanted to beat him up, both.

"Hi," I said. "What are you doing?"

He turned around but didn't answer. His braces glittered and there were leaves in his hair. My hilarity increased. I grinned wildly at the book titles on the shelves behind him. They were a tattered lot, paperback romance novels and westerns crammed in beside classics and handprinted first editions. One whole row, I noticed, was filled with medical texts; Suzanne's second husband had been a psychiatrist.

"What if something is wrong with me?" he asked.

"What? What are you talking about? Nothing's wrong with you."

"You're sure of that?"

"Yes." I was. "You're fine. Just a little...unfinished."

"Unfinished." He breathed roughly, glaring. "Like a symphony?"

"More like furniture."

He threw his head back and laughed. His braces glittered and the rubber bands in his mouth gleamed like little ropes, holding his small teeth in bondage. The end of the hallway darkened and Suzanne stood there, clapping her hands together. "How does she do it?" she cried to the others. "He hasn't cracked a smile or said a word to me all week!" I ducked my head, stiff, as Suzanne hugged me, her nails digging into my back, and when I freed myself, Pierre, again, had gone.

"He used to be a chess master," I told Carter as we drove home that night. "He quit because he doesn't like to compete. He's a fencer too. And he's studied ballet. Right now he's designing a new kind of kite you can attach like a sail to racing motorcycles."

"He's a creep," Carter said.

That word stung me, not because it was cruel, but because it was true. The way Pierre slid around on his black canvas shoes, standing behind me sometimes when I did not know he was there, the way his breath rasped through his wet silver braces. The pale damp of his skin. Insect, grub, maggot, creep. I could see all that. He did not seem to know how to use his mystery, or his beauty, or his sorrow enough, it seemed to me. I saw it. How could others be so blind? Suzanne's children treated him as if he were their servant; he didn't object when they plucked his wallet from his pocket and ran howling from the room. On the evenings when she wasn't bemoaning his coldness, his depressions, his neglect, Suzanne spoke of Pierre as if he were for sale, boasting that he was as helpful as a woman with cooking, cleaning, and garden work. "He does all the children's laundry. He even sews the buttons back on their jammies," she said once. I glanced over at Pierre, ready to share his shame at this, but he was staring quietly down at the cat on his lap. He was quiet too the night his brother came to dinner. The brother, a Toronto architect named Marc, told stories on Pierre that were supposed to be funny, but even Carter was willing to change the subject after twenty minutes of hearing about the time Pierre dropped Marc's Leica into the Grand Canyon, crashed Marc's Porsche in Big Sur, lost Marc's credit cards in Reno. "In *Reno!*" Marc roared, shaking his head.

"You're not like your brother," I murmured, over coffee, as Pierre helped himself to the strawberries on my dessert plate.

"Maybe that's what's wrong with me," Pierre said. His hand trembled over my plate and he shot me that dim sweet smile I was starting to look for and miss in Carter's range of expressions. I had been starting to think of Pierre more and more lately; it was like cheap music playing inside me, sometimes loud, sometimes soft, but constant. I knew what to expect because I'd gone through this with Carter, too, at first; I knew it would fade. It's just a crush, I told myself. Smoke and mirrors—nothing more. I rose to make black coffee for Suzanne. Pierre was standing in the hallway listening to the children fight upstairs. His head was tipped, his mouth was slack, his shirt—could it be?—yes, his shirt was buttoned backward.

I don't know whose idea it was to dance. But one night, in that summer of drunken dinners at Suzanne's house, one of the engineers rolled back all the rugs in the living room, and the other went upstairs and bargained with the children for some of their cassettes. Suzanne led off with the basketball coach, the engineers broke into an orderly fox trot, and Carter lasted ten full minutes with the ex-gymnast before passing out on one of Suzanne's brocade armchairs. I looked for Pierre and finally glimpsed him, hovering like a delicate insect at the periphery of his own party; when I beckoned he walked toward me with his eyes down. His touch was light on my waist. His fingers were sleek and cool, webbed between the thumb and palm. He smelled like apricots and ink. He was perfectly poised and on beat and his erection was so high and horizontal it felt like a ruler between us; once, when it brushed my skirt, he said, "Excuse me." He twirled me as if I were the young queen of love and at the end of the dance he leaned forward and kissed me on the cheek with a tiny popping sound from his bands that was at once the most intimate and the most comical sound I had ever heard.

In the morning I woke up edgy with guilt and distrust and a thunderous hangover. I replayed the low groan Pierre had given when I'd pressed myself against him; my stomach clenched with self-hate and a slow, delighted lust. I looked at the little rooms of the little house Carter owned and the stylish functional furnishings he had bought before I knew him. I looked at Carter himself—showered and combed and already deep in the sports section of the Sunday paper. "Is this the way we're going to live forever?" I asked. Carter looked up at me cheerfully. "I hope so," he said, "don't you like it?" I shook my head. "Poor Boopsy," he said and went back to his paper.

I knew where Pierre worked; I'd looked up the phone number. One autumn afternoon, when the light coming through the living room was so grey I could feel myself thinning to transparency inside it, I walked to the phone and called him. "Who?" said the man who answered. I repeated the name. A few minutes later Pierre came to the phone. He sounded hoarse and winded and I thought of his wild eyes, their ill, muddy look, the way his hair lay limp on his neck. I took a deep breath. "Hi," I said. "Do you want to have lunch some time?"

There was a long pause. I could hear him breathe. I waited a little longer and then I hung up. He did not call back.

A few days later Suzanne invited Carter and me to a costume party for Halloween. I was about to lie and say we couldn't go when she began to cry. "I'm losing my mind," she said. "Pierre drags around like he's dying. He won't eat, he won't sleep; he just sits and stares. I've talked to the kids' therapist, and she says," here she paused to blow her nose, "that Pierre's a classic case of passive dependent and either he's suicidal or in love and it doesn't matter because I have to save myself. I really do. I give too much to people who don't give back; I always have; that's how I am."

My heart was racing. *In love*—could he be? Not eating? Not sleeping? I sat at my sewing table, curtain material spilling from my lap. I saw for the first time that the little house around me was neither a jail nor a haven but a place I could leave.

We went to the party as Prince Charming and Cinderella. I made Carter a velvet cape and a crown out of tinfoil and for myself, as penance, I sewed a patchwork skirt of old curtain scraps. I wore scuffed wooden clogs, tucked my hair under a kerchief, smudged charcoal on my cheeks. But my eyes were too bright to meet in the mirror and the tap of my foot as Carter circled the block looking for the best place to park was not, I knew, the dance of a virgin.

The party was enormous, much bigger than usual. Guests spilled out into the backyard and laughed under the moonlight. The children ran wild. Suzanne's other husbands were there, someone said, but no one knew who they were; everyone was in costume. The two engineers had dressed up as tennis rackets. The ex-gymnast was a gorilla; the basketball coach wore a wet suit and snorkel. Suzanne was a gypsy, with even more flowers in her hair and bracelets than usual, and Pierre was nowhere to be found.

"Go upstairs," Suzanne urged, "and force him to come down."

I looked back at Carter. He was talking to the coach; his crown sat neatly on his sleek combed head. He blew me a kiss across the room and waved, a small wave: good-bye.

I had never been upstairs in that house before. I paused on each step. I looked out the hall window at the street below where Pierre's old truck was parked. I passed the children's bedroom, a foreign barracks of bunk beds. Something plastic broke underfoot and the white cat crept out of an opened closet and twined around my ankle. I picked it up, heard it hiss, felt its spine twist, hard, in my hands, and set it down. At last I came to the closed bedroom door. I knocked very lightly. "Pierre?" I said. "Are you sulking?"

There was no answer. I opened the door. The room was dark but I could see him on the bed. He was still in his work clothes—a T-shirt, greasy jeans; he still had his boots on. His lips were parted in a slim silver smile, and his eyes were open too, looking straight at me. They took me in, those eyes of his; they shone on me, and spoke. Here you are, they said. At last. Let's go.

Beginning Lessons

IT'S THEIR LAST DAY IN MEXICO and Harriet is *muy feliciando*. No. Wrong. What sort of word is *feliciando*? She ducks her head and studies the two iguana masks it is her turn to carry; they are balanced on top of the backpack on her lap and gently scratch her sunburned arms as the minivan bounces from one pothole to another on its way out of the city toward the airport. *Feliciando* sounds like something she might have made up; she's been doing that, lately: faking it. "Happy?" Ben asks. She looks across the aisle at him, startled. That's the word.

"How did you know?" she asks.

Ben grins and snaps her picture. Harriet sticks her tongue out, too late. Ben turns to the man beside him and opens his phrase book. He likes factual questions, ones that can be answered with numbers. What is the population of your city? What is the elevation? On and on. Yawn and yawn.

Harriet leans against the torn vinyl seat and tries to look out the window but the glass is so smudged it scarcely lets light through. It almost looks licked. She remembers the pilgrims Ben photographed kissing the glass case of saints' relics in the old stone cathedral. What were they praying for? She frowns, recalling their rush of quick, soft Spanish. In two weeks, she thinks, I have said only two words: *No comprendo*. And half the time I can't remember those.

"Hon?" She looks up as the van brakes to a stop and sees the man Ben was talking to leaning above her. "He's getting off here," Ben says, "and he wants to know your name before he leaves."

"I can't say my name," Harriet reminds him.

"Try." Ben's expression is as good-humored as ever but his voice is tight. Drop the h, Harriet reminds herself, roll the rr's, do a diphthong with the ie: try. Her name, made Spanish, is all air, shrill as a curse word. The man leans closer, his breath rich with breakfast and Chiclets.

"He wants you to ask his name now," Ben prompts.

Harriet looks at the man's face, sweating faintly, at the expectant glint of gold teeth. Her head crowds with inappropriate noises then stills, utterly empty. She played the Spanish tapes Ben gave her for her birthday but she never really studied them, and the nights she was supposed to go to the conversation class were the nights she was meeting her company's sales manager in a hotel room, downtown. She raises her eyes and opens her mouth. What comes out is not Spanish, nor English, but high school French. "*Alors*," she says to the man. "*J'regrette.*"

The man straightens, pleased, and waves as he leaves.

"Thanks a lot," Harriet says to Ben when he's gone. "You did that on purpose."

Ben looks genuinely hurt by this. "I'm just trying to help you out. You'll never learn unless you try." He waits. "Right?"

Harriet shrugs. She knows he'll say "Right?" again—and again—until she nods, and she knows too that she will eventually nod. Because he is right. Ridiculous as he is, with his camera and straw hat and bright tourist T-shirt, Ben is right. He has been bold and curious and playful on this trip and she has been shy and fearful and wrong. She has mispronounced everything, of course, but she's also misread maps and lost luggage. She's eschewed the drinking water but thirstily sucked the ice; she's been sick from insect bites and coral cuts and diarrhea and sunburn; she's been punishing herself, she knows it; what she hasn't known is why. She broke off with the sales manager weeks ago. I should be rewarded, she thinks. I made the right choice. I saved his marriage and I saved my own. I should be forgiven for...*sinning* is the word she comes up with, but *sinning* seems too strong for the weary erotic wrestling she and the sales manager engaged in, week after week.

The van starts up with a lurch and she grabs for the masks before they slide to the floor. They are papier-mache; Ben bought them at a street stand last night. Both are ugly; the trick is to decide which is the ugliest. One is a blue iguana with a hand sticking out of its forehead. The other is a yellow frog with an iguana rolling out of its mouth. This one reminds Harriet of herself, of the way she's been feeling lately. She holds the mask to her face, inhales its cheap resin scent, and drops it back on her lap.

When she looks up she sees that a well-dressed young woman with a briefcase has taken the seat next to Ben. The woman flashes a blank, radiant smile at both of them, and Ben, straightening, smiles back. Here goes, Harriet thinks. He's about to make another "contact with the people." She turns back to the window. She can see her own reflection, pale and wavery. She looks young and drowned, like someone floating underwater. She feels as if she's under water. Feverish, remote, detached. She shakes her head and presses her fingers to her tired ears. Someone behind her opens a newspaper; the rustle it makes reminds her again of water. She thinks of the little lake she and Ben hiked to a few days ago. On clear days, Ben had told her, you could actually look down through the lake and see an entire village below—it was all there, the church, the bank, the bare branches of the plane trees in the square. It had been flooded twenty years ago by the government for a dam and it still stood, intact. Harriet had tried to see through the water but it was a dull, overcast afternoon and the top of the lake was opaque with scum. Above them, buzzards had watched from the cliffs. "Everything in Mexico," she had complained, "looks good until you get up close," and Ben had said, calmly, "That's true of most things, don't you think?"

She wants to lean forward now and say, "What did you mean?" but Ben is chatting with the woman with the briefcase and anyway he'd deny he meant anything. She could have had five affairs and Ben wouldn't have noticed. No, that's not fair, she amends. Ben is a good man. He just doesn't see things. He is asking the same old questions about population and industry that he asks everyone and the woman is responding as everyone has, politely, and with pleasure. How nice these people are, Harriet thinks. Too nice. It's exhausting. She listens to Ben say he thinks Mexico is *muy interesante* and feels a rush of despair and affection and envy; he is, at least, talking.

The woman is unusual looking, for a Mexican, with pale, mushroom-colored skin and a large unlipsticked mouth. Her dark hair is chopped short and curls close to her head. Her ringless hands twist on the embossed leather lid of her briefcase as she listens to Ben, and her eyes still have that intense, expectant sparkle that Harriet saw when she first stepped into the van. "I notice you like to speak my language," the woman is saying, "but I speak English if you prefer."

Harriet leans back and closes her eyes. She hopes that whatever they speak they will not speak very loudly. She has been up since four and feels the full weight of her weariness now. The church bells this morning next to their hotel sounded off-key and jangled, as if they were being played by a tantrumming child, and then the roosters, with their hoarse, reckless, strangle-me-now screams in the dark. What will it be like at home? she wonders. Quiet, of course. She can see their bedroom waiting: the white spread, the skylight beaded with drops of grey Seattle rain, the exercise bike and rowing machine gleaming like hospital equipment in the gloom. There will be no message from the sales manager on the answering machine, no little pornographic poems in the mailbox. She tries to feel sad about this but the sad thing is that she feels nothing at all.

"Hon?"

Harriet looks up.

"She's speaking to you," Ben gestures to the woman beside him.

"Do you speak English?" the woman repeats.

"I used to," Harriet says. "I'm not sure I speak anything anymore."

Ben clucks his tongue. He wants Harriet to be what he calls her "real self" when she meets people—warm, natural, two things Harriet is touched he thinks she is or ever could be—but the woman leans forward and, breathless, says, "I know what it is like to be silent for too long. I know how that feels. You get all locked up inside. At first you want to talk, then no you don't want to talk, then pretty soon you don't even want to try. You just want to be left alone in your cave! To suffer! But that isn't good for you, to stay locked up in silence. That can really hurt you. Because we are all people, right, brothers and sisters? And we need to talk to each other and say, Hey! I am here! You are too! Let's be happy together!"

Harriet stares. Oh, brother, she thinks. She glances at Ben, but Ben is in love. This woman—girl, really—is exactly who he'd like Harriet to be. Fresh, innocent, open. Harriet is surprised by the quick, deep bite of jealousy this stranger makes her feel.

"I notice you," the girl says, shaking a finger at Harriet, "living in a cave. But you will feel better as soon as you start to talk to other people."

"That's what I've been telling her," Ben says, radiant. "All she has to do is try."

"Just try," the girl agrees.

They beam at Harriet and Harriet shrugs. It is quiet for a minute, and then the girl—who introduces herself as Ariella? Gabriella? something quick and soft—begins to tell Ben about her three years in the United States as a college student, the fun she had with her girlfriends, the American boys she dated. Harriet yawns and taps the masks in her lap. Used to drifting out of conversations in Spanish, she soon drifts out of this one as well. It is so easy not to listen. It is a little gift. The thought of gifts makes her remember the embroidered pouch of amber beads she bought herself last night, as a present for her new pure life. They had been in a display case, the price clearly marked, and she had not had to barter. What a relief it had been, to simply point and pay. Of course they might not be real amber. That is a possibility. They might be plastic, or glass. She slips her hand into her purse, pulls out the pouch, and cautiously spills the contents into her palm. Oh, hell, she mouths to herself. The salesgirl in the shop made a mistake. Instead of the long rope of honey-colored beads, she must have taken out the pendant that was displayed in the case beside them. Oh, ugh, Harriet thinks. She hates this pendant, a lump of cola-colored stuff with an actual—she looks closer—dead bug of some sort inside it. She hates the pendant and she hates herself. Why didn't she pay attention? Why did she look away when she should have been watching what the salesgirl was doing? Her disappointment in the pendant releases a hive of other hurts that have stung her recently and she darkens, remembering the street boy who cursed her quickly from a doorway, the dead dog she bent to pet in the street, the baby with sores on its eyes lying sick in its mother's shawl. "I notice you are back in your cave," the young woman says.

Harriet has had it with picturesque speech. "I bought the wrong damn thing," she says.

"You did?" Ben, clear-eyed, peers at her. "What'd you buy, hon?" He takes the pendant she hands him, turns it over, and hands it to the young woman.

"But it's very beautiful," the young woman says. "It is a fossil. You know that? Many hundreds—thousands—millions! of years ago this insect he was just traveling along, you know, like you and me, clump clump clump, eating his flowers and flying his wings and then he lands on this tree all covered with gold, he thinks it is blossoms, he thinks it is honey, and suddenly he can't move, he's stuck, and the sun it goes down and he gets more and more tired and pretty soon he says, 'Oh, well I'll go to sleep' and here he is now." She hands the amber back to Ben, who fingers it respectfully and gives it back to Harriet with a pleased steady look.

"Are you a teacher?" Harriet asks, her voice as toneless as she can make it without sounding rude. "You sound like someone who spends a lot of time with children."

"No. I am too big a child myself. Don't you think? You think: a little. Well, you are right." The girl laughs and smoothes out her skirt. "I would like to teach children, though, someday. I would like to do some good in the world. That is why we are here, don't you think? What do you do?"

"Ben's an engineer," Harriet says briefly, dropping the amber back in its pouch. "I work in publishing."

"Ah, yes, but what do you *do*? For the world?"

"Not as much as we'd like to," Ben says. "That's for sure." He clears his throat. "So. Where are you flying to today?"

"Oh, I cannot afford to fly anymore," the girl says. "It is so expensive, it is only for rich people."

"We're not rich," Ben protests. "Even with both of us working, we don't have much money..."

"Oh, yes, money. I know about money! You know what I would do if I had money? I would give it away!"

"You have to have it to give it," Ben agrees.

"Yes. I used to have a great deal of money, when I worked. But now..." She lifts her hands and shrugs. Her skirt, Harriet notices, while well-cut, is thin from many washings, and the cuffs of her jacket are frayed.

"So you're between jobs?" Ben asks.

"I had a job, yes. But it was bad. My bosses were bad. You had to watch every word you said because if they didn't like it, or they didn't agree with you, out you would go; they would not let you stay even in the same building with them."

"And you're too independent for that," Ben says.

"Yes. I am too independent to make money! I am too independent to be rich! But I don't care. I just like to be happy! Don't you like to be happy?"

"It's hard to be happy," Ben says.

"Very hard," the girl agrees. "But when I am not happy, you know what I do? I go to bed! I sleep for three, maybe four days. And when I wake up, everything is normal again."

"Three or four days?" Ben repeats. "That's a long time."

"Yes." The girl nods brightly. "Sometimes it takes a long time to get normal."

Harriet stares. The girl is pale but strong boned, and with a strong glow. She does not look like she has ever been sick.

"So you quit your job," Ben continues. "That takes a lot of courage, to just quit and walk out."

"Yes," says the girl. "Well I did not quit, no. They fired me."

"Because those crazy bosses didn't like you?"

"No," the girl says. "Because I was crazy myself." She laughs again and lifts her head. And suddenly Harriet sees something she has not seen before—a jagged white scar across the girl's throat. "I had many problems," the girl explains, "with my nerves."

"Nerves," Ben repeats. He glances at Harriet, who frowns at him, hard. The frown hasn't worked in the past, when she has tried to pull him out of endless conversations with silver vendors and hammock salesmen, but it seems to work now. Ben doesn't say any more.

"I was sick with nerves for a long time," the girl continues. She touches her throat and Harriet watches her fingers tiptoe across the long line of the scar. "I saw things, terrible things, you cannot imagine the things I saw. Worse than those masks! Much worse than that! And I heard things too, voices, bad voices, saying to do...bad things to myself. It was as if I was inside"—she leans forward and presses her hand to the smudged glass of Harriet's window—"and outside too. I could not reach myself. I could not pull myself through. Do you know what I am saying?"

"Yes," says Harriet.

"Yes," says the girl. "And then Jesus came one day and helped me and that is why I love Jesus so much—you love Jesus don't you?"

Jesus? Harriet doesn't know what to say. She feels as if a door has just been shut in her face. She turns with familiar relief as Ben finally looks up from the camera he has been fiddling with and speaks for them both. "We respect him as a teacher," Ben says. His voice is flat, his eyes are far away.

"A teacher? Oh, yes, a fine, a wonderful, a beautiful teacher! But also a savior! You must love Jesus as a savior?"

"We don't believe in God," Ben says, patting his pocket for a fresh roll of film.

"You don't..." the girl twists her hands and looks down at her lap, close to tears. "I am so sorry," she says. She starts to open her briefcase. "You must let me give you some books, you must let me help," she begins, but Ben interrupts, "No thanks. We're really not interested. And look. We're at the airport already."

Harriet looks up, as surprised as she's been by anything on this trip to see the terminal shimmering before them. She gathers her things and, with a weak wave to the girl, who is praying, actually praying, follows Ben across the parking lot.

"Whew," Ben says, as he opens the door of the airport. "Imagine coming all this way just to run into a Born Again. I guess people are crazy all over." Then his voice softens. "Poor kid," he says. "Did you see that scar?"

"I did. I kept wondering how she got it."

"Maybe she tried to cut her own throat."

"Can you do that?"

Ben is suddenly impatient. "How should I know?" he says. "You always think I know things I don't."

Harriet waits. What *do* you know? she wants to ask. And when will you tell me? But all she says is: "Did you catch her name?"

"No."

Harriet stands behind him as he checks in their baggage. He is talking to the man behind the desk about their flight—what gate they should go to, what time they will leave. She listens to his slow stumble through Spanish and hears nothing but the exhaustion and—what else? Yes—the disappointment in his voice. He wants to believe, she thinks, like I do. He wants to believe that people can be sweet and funny without being crippled or crazy; he wants to believe that lovers can be faithful and that there truly is a way we can—what had the poor girl said?—do good in the world. Because that's what matters. Isn't that why I ended that stupid affair after all? To do good? To be good? To try?

She shivers and looks up. The ceiling is not yet finished in this new airport and there are squares of sky between the crossed steel beams. It could flood here, she thinks. It could flood anywhere. She imagines clear, quiet, killing waters pouring in through the roof and feels the old kick of panic; my life, she thinks, what is happening to my life? She twists around to see the girl standing just outside the door with her briefcase open on the sidewalk before her. A flash of light from a passing cab's mirror sparks off the girl's head and for a moment she is impossibly framed in a halo. Harriet touches Ben's shoulder, says, "Be right back," and turns toward the door.

The girl does not look so young in the sunlight. There are a few strands of grey in her hair and olive colored bruises beneath her bright eyes. She is not the sort of person I talk to, Harriet thinks. Ever. She is the sort of person I avoid.

"I would like to say good-bye," she says. "I enjoyed meeting you and I felt I understood some of the things you told us." The girl holds a placard neatly printed with Bible verses in four languages in her hand and Harriet is careful not to look at it. "I would also like to learn to say your name."

The girl smiles her sudden luminous smile at this. "What will you do when you learn it?" she asks.

"I don't know," Harriet admits.

"Will you learn another name? And another? Will you learn the name of Our Father and Jesus and..."

"Come on," Harriet interrupts. She shields her eyes and squints as a jet roars off from the airfield behind them.

"Well," the girl says, her voice high and sweet and relentlessly happy, "we will have to start somewhere with you I guess." She opens her mouth. And Harriet listens.

The Blessed Among Us

AMONG HER OTHER TALENTS, Iona sees ghosts. We have already
heard about the dead Indian in the blanket who came up behind her at a
campground in Utah; now, in the middle of her own party, when she should
be mingling with other, more important, guests, Iona tells us about the child
who sat on the back stairs of an old house she and Dean lived in when they
were going to law school. The child was shy and never looked up, and she
was dressed so oddly, in ruffled skirts and boots, that at first they thought
she belonged to the religious commune on the corner. It wasn't until Iona
and Dean had passed their bar exams and were getting ready to buy their
first apartment that they learned the child had been seen sitting there, off
and on, since 1906. "Believe me," Iona says.

We do. We always have. We are members of Iona's writing group and
we believe every word she says. All of us tell stories and some of us tell lies,
but Iona never lies; she doesn't need to; her life—all the reviewers are saying this—is as interesting as her fiction. There are questions we would like
to ask about the little booted ghost—what color hair she had, and what she
died of, and if you could touch her when you held out your hand—but the
party is roaring and surging around us and Iona, with a last bright look, is
pulled away. We sip our champagne, lick strawberry juice off our fingertips,
take a bite of white meringue cake, and tell each other how nice we look.
"It's just a little odd," Joelle points out, "that we're all wearing green."

We stop to consider this. Green, the color of jealousy. It doesn't mean a thing. We could have worn black. In the front room, a pianist tinkles through the score of *Les Misérables*. That doesn't mean anything either. Nancy's jade earrings bring out her eyes; Joelle's shamrock pendant is the last gift her husband bought her before he died; my velvet beret came from a thrift shop downtown. We have a tendency, we know it, to nitpick, to focus on details and lose sight of themes. One day, we predict, we will start to critique each other's lives, as well as stories, and then where will we be.

Hopefully here, in Iona's apartment, where we have been meeting for three years. The apartment looks different tonight—festive—it's the balloons, we decide, the balloons and crepe streamers with Iona's name printed on them. Children are already tangled in the crepe, one couple is trying to dance, the caterers are pushing through the crowd with silver trays held high. Despite the festivity, or perhaps because of it, we feel tired tonight, Joelle and Nancy and I; we don't know why; it's been a hard week. Joelle lost her lease, Nancy's wallet was stolen, I had my car towed at work—minor things, but they add up. We almost didn't come, we say, but now we're glad we did. Glad for ourselves, and glad for Iona. Especially glad for Iona. Iona's novel has only been out a month and it is already fourth on the *New York Times* Best Seller list. "Fourth and going up," her former law partner told me as I came in the door. "Can you believe it?"

"Yes," I'd said. I never had liked this man, James.

"Don't give me yes." James had leaned toward me, grinning. "You girls must be shitting bricks."

Iona pauses before us again with her head tipped, smiling. She introduces us to a Cuban novelist we have all long admired. We stare at the novelist, a beautiful woman, heavily made up, with a diamond crucifix at her throat. We have already met a Black poet and a Japanese playwright tonight; both of them were beautiful too, and both, we were alarmed to see, looked about our age, or younger.

"My group," Iona breathes. "I was just telling them about that ghost."

"Oh, yes!" the novelist nods, her eyes skimming our faces. We freeze, attentive. This woman, too, we know has seen ghosts. She has written about them, ancestral spirits who drift through the bougainvillea at dusk. She can see entire folk histories in them. But what can she see in us? Before we are given a clue, she is swept away by a tall man in a pink leather jacket, and Iona herself is engulfed in the thick freckled arms of her agent, KayBeth.

"Iona! At last! There's someone here you need to meet!" KayBeth's arms part to reveal a bald smiling man in suede who peeps, like a baby bird in a nest, "Hi!Hi!Hi!" We nod back but the man is not greeting us. His eyes have not left Iona's face.

Nor should they. Iona really does look lovely tonight. She has in fact looked lovely for months, ever since her book first sold. A visible luminescence, like a pearly powder, has settled on her skin. Her teeth seem whiter, her eyes seem clearer, her full lips have a redness we do not remember from a year ago. Maybe it was there, and we never saw—but no—it's new. There is a quiet decisive shimmer to Iona that is new. Star quality, we decide. Iona was always attractive—as a lawyer for one of the largest firms in the city she had to be—and even when she left the law firm to stay home and write her novel she dressed well, in a writerly way, in big sweaters and sweats, but now, since her book has come out, to such rave reviews, she is truly stunning. She has started to wear her hair back in a sleek neat knot with brilliant clips on her tiny, almost childlike ears. For the publicity photos in *People* and *Newsweek* she wore her mother's bird feather headdress, but for her party tonight she is wearing a pewter-colored cape with built out shoulders; it is made of some stiff wrinkled silk that rustles when she moves. There is a moonstone pendant around her neck and a flat taffeta bow crowns her knot of blond hair. Anyone else—Nancy, or Joelle, or I—would look ridiculous, dressed like this, but Iona looks like a winged insect in a designer chrysalis, about to hatch. Her eyes are bright and light tonight, and wild. When she says "Hi" back to the little man, her scaffolded shoulders tremble and sway and he seems to levitate toward her uplifted hand.

"You three," KayBeth says, turning the full force of her professional beam on us as we clump, cake plates in hand, to one side. "You three are just who I want to see. Let's leave Iona alone with her publicist for a minute, shall we; they just have to talk about her tour of Europe and whether it should include Italy or not; what do you think, should our Iona go to Italy in May? It gets sooo hot, but come with me, come on now, just down the hall; I have something for you. Presents!"

Docile, we follow KayBeth down the narrow hall to the bedrooms. We have to thread our way through thickly packed guests—secretaries and law clerks from Iona's old office and two shortstops and the third baseman from Dean's softball team. Everyone seems to raise the same dark stare as we pass; the trapped-animal party look, compounded by drink and self-consciousness and perhaps by envy of Iona as well, for everyone seems to be saying the same thing.

"She deserved it," they are saying. "If anyone ever deserved a bestseller, Iona did. Look at what she went through with that mother of hers. It's amazing she ever survived."

"Want to bet we're getting T-shirts?" Nancy whispers as we edge down the hall. "Want to bet KayBeth bought us something as tacky as T-shirts with her colossal commission?"

Just because KayBeth didn't take your book, I think—but do not say. Joelle, Nancy, and I are not—KayBeth's words—"ready yet." Joelle has been working on a long novel about her husband's struggle with leukemia. Nancy has finished a collection of very short stories she calls "pre-stories"—last year she sold one to a magazine in Canada. I wrote a book of poetry that won a national prize three years ago; since then I have been trying to cross over into fiction, without much success, although I can tell I am getting better because my rejection forms have hand-signed signatures on them now, which Iona, who has never had a rejection form in her life, insists is a good sign.

KayBeth leads us into Dean and Iona's bedroom and reaches under the walnut dresser, tugging out a bag of T-shirts, which she spills out on the bed. "Only three left," she says. "Isn't this lucky? Of course," she looks up, beaming, "everything connected to Iona's wonderful wonderful book has been so lucky." She smiles down at the T-shirts. "Sam Shepard and Jessica Lange both loved these to bits; they said they would wear them every day on their ranch. Sting wears his to bed." We lift our eyes and stare at her. "Didn't you hear about Sting?" she says. "He wants to make a movie of her book."

"I thought Jane Fonda wanted to make a movie of her book," Joelle says, sulky.

"Yes, Jane is definitely interested. But, girls. *Sting.*"

We are silent. Stung. We accept the T-shirts. They are gold with the name of Iona's book, *The Blessed Among Us,* in loopy silver script, and they are all size small, Iona's size. We look at the photos of Dean's family on one wall of the bedroom and at Iona's rare butterfly collection on the other. There is a framed cartoon above the bed of a woman sobbing "Oh, *No!* I Forgot To Have *Children!*" A large china doll stares from the seat of the exercise bike in the corner. Orchids from Iona's publisher overflow the tabletops and crowd the windowsills. A huge vase of white roses sits on the dresser.

KayBeth watches us watching Iona's things. Her eyes are, for a second, uncharacteristically soft. "Don't feel sorry for us," Nancy warns her. "We'll make it," I say. "In our own time," Joelle adds. "In our own way." We do not look at KayBeth as we speak and she does not acknowledge that we have spoken at all; perhaps we have not. Her eyes blink and sharpen.

"So girls," she says, "what do you think of Iona's success?"

"Wonderful," Joelle says.

"Just wonderful," Nancy says.

"She really deserved it," I add.

KayBeth agrees, without effort, without irony. "She really did," KayBeth nods. "The thing about Iona is...she's so nice. So many people in this business just aren't nice. Don't you think Iona's nice?"

"Really nice," we say.

"And talented," KayBeth continues.

"Really talented," we agree.

"And what do you think of her new book? The one she's just started working on?"

We hesitate. Iona's first book was a fictionalized autobiography of her childhood growing up in the Brazilian jungle; it told how she discovered her father's suicide and lived with her mother's drug addiction until she was able to escape with her brother to California where she put herself through law school. This new one also is set in Brazil, but it's a spy novel and it seems—to us—despite all Iona's careful research, less moving than the first book, with too many characters and a trite plot and not enough of what Nancy calls "the good stuff"—magic and passion and violence and joy.

"It's slow," Joelle says. "So far."

"A little hard to follow," I add.

"You girls are so mean," KayBeth scolds. "I swear if you three were still critiquing Iona's last book it wouldn't even be published yet."

There's truth to this. Iona herself has said we are her harshest critics. Still, the exasperation in KayBeth's voice surprises us. We aren't that hard on Iona. And look how kind the critics have been. There has not been one single negative review. "The only bad thing about this book," one reviewer wrote, "is that it ends." Nancy called early one Sunday morning to read that one to me on the phone. We both said Wow, made gagging noises, and then laughed. What could we do? We said, "Good for Iona." We are saying it still. Aren't we saying it loud enough for KayBeth to hear?

"I think the new book is going to be even more exciting than the first," KayBeth predicts. "I expect a big hit."

We look at each other. Has Iona been showing her new book to KayBeth? In rough draft? Why? KayBeth is a businesswoman, not a writer. She can tell

Iona what will sell, but she cannot tell Iona, as we can, what will break a reader's heart, and what will heal it back. If Iona is writing for KayBeth, Iona is writing for money. And no one writes well for money. This is something we believe, although, to be fair, we have not had a chance to find out.

"A big hit," KayBeth repeats. Her voice has a firm, formidable resonance and her stubby freckled hands fold on her hips as she faces us down. Before she became an agent, we remember, KayBeth was headmistress of a girls' school; despite ourselves we act like schoolgirls now, shuffling our feet, fighting the urge to giggle and bolt.

"What I cannot get over," a bearded man says from the doorway, in a voice like church chimes, "is that the market is ready for the product at exactly the same time the product is ready for the market. That seems to me a miracle."

"It is," KayBeth says. "It is absolutely a miracle." The man in the doorway and KayBeth nod together; they seem to know each other well. "These are the girls," KayBeth explains. "Iona's little group."

"Then you know Dean," the man says. "Tell me. How do you think Dean will do?"

"Do?" we repeat.

"In New York. You know. Do you think he'll hold up? At parties? With people?"

No one holds up at parties, I think. With people. I excuse myself. I am going to need an aspirin, several aspirin, and I know Iona keeps them in the kitchen cupboard, above the sink. I tuck my T-shirt close to my side and escape down the hall again. There is a man in rumpled chinos standing in a corner of the kitchen and for a second I don't recognize him. "Dean?" I say. He looks up from his coffee mug and blinks.

"Oh. Hi." He looks exhausted. "Have you met Benjamin?" He gestures to a man slumped on the floor by his feet.

"Yes," I say. "I know Benjamin." Benjamin is Iona's first husband; his present wife used to be married to Dean. The papers somehow don't know this yet; even *People* overlooked it—another example of Iona's luck. Benjamin looks as tired as Dean and although he leans back against the cupboard nonchalantly and blows smoke rings toward the orchids on the table, there is something of the bum about him, something of the bum about them both. I am struck again by how much they look alike, these two, with their rough brush cuts and patient doggy eyes. They seem married to each other in a way neither of them has ever seemed married to Iona, a truer couple somehow.

"You know what happened today?" Dean lifts slow eyes. "I was at a lunch counter downtown and this middle-aged woman came up to me and said, 'Oh, are you the husband of that writer I read about in the Sunday paper last week?' "

I wait, but that's the end of the story. Dean's not a raconteur. His stories have never made much sense but no one's minded because Dean himself is so good-natured and likable. Lately, though, I've noticed that Iona starts to hum whenever Dean talks; it's probably unconscious on her part but it's as if she's putting some sort of soft melodic gag over his mouth. Maybe Dean won't *do* in New York after all. Benjamin, yawning on the floor, doesn't look like he'll do much better. I think of Iona's hand, raised above the levitating little man and see again how trembly she was, like a child carried away with its own performance. What must it be like for her? I wonder. Waking up every morning as if it were Christmas. Knowing everyone loves her, and the work she does. Able to buy anything she wants—anything she sees in a magazine or a shop window. If I were fourth on the bestseller list and going, as James claimed, up—what would I do? I would pay off my debts and quit my job, but other than that? I cannot imagine. Yes I can. I would sit hunched over a keyboard in a quiet room putting one small word after another until I had told every story I knew. What a strange way to live! I look up, marveling. Dean is still talking.

"At first," he tells me, "I figured that all this publicity and all this money was Iona's thing and she'd handle it, you know, like she's handled everything else. But it's sort of out of hand now. It's gotten out of hand. Of course," he adds, his voice low, "it's very exciting too."

"If you like fame and fortune," Benjamin says.

"Yeah." Dean laughs without opening his mouth. "That's it. If you like fame and fortune." He shakes his head. "You wouldn't believe the phone calls," he says. "You wouldn't believe the mail."

I wait, but that, once more, is all. I find the aspirin and a glass. Looking through the kitchen window I am surprised to see Iona's cat, Hissyfit, sitting on the outside sill. Hissy is an evil cat, skinny, ill, riddled with fleas, but she is always indulged and given the run of the house. At the weekly writers' meetings she yowls to come in, yowls to go out, yowls as she leaps into our laps to spit up her pills. Why is she locked out tonight? Perhaps she, like Dean and Benjamin, no longer will do. She bares her teeth at me; I bare mine back. As I set my glass down, I see Iona's mother sitting, ignored, in the little pantry off the kitchen. I smile at her and she smiles back and makes an airy sign with one hand in the air—the sign, I realize, of someone holding a pencil and writing. She has probably made that same gesture all night to anyone who asks about Iona. My daughter the little writer. Always scribbling scribbling. She drops her hand and sinks back, her face blank and unlined, one high-topped canvas athletic shoe poking out beneath her white robes. After her husband hung himself from the mast of his yacht, Iona's mother took Iona and the boy and fled up the river to a native village where she lived off peyote for two years; she kept herself and her children naked most of that time, Iona wrote, and fed them raw meat from bird traps she set herself. "She believes she has a guardian angel," Iona explained in a recent interview. "She always said that I had one too." I watch her now as she serenely swallows a yawn. Her boyfriend, a twenty-six-year-old tour guide she met in Tulum, stands behind her and rubs her shoulders.

"If I had a mother like Iona's," I hear one guest say to another as I make my way back down the hall to the front rooms where the party still rages, the piano still plays, "I'd be a writer too."

"She didn't have to make anything up," the other guest agrees.

"That's right. It was all handed to her."

"Hey!" It's James, exactly as drunk, no more no less, as he was an hour ago at the door. "Don't I know you? I know you. You're Iona's newest best friend."

"Guess again." I try to slide by him.

"Newest old friend," he corrects. "So tell me, friend, have you read her book? You have? You're in the minority in this house, friend; in fact, you may be the only one here besides me and our lovely hostess who has actually read the damn thing. So," he grabs my arm and holds it, "what did you think of it? Because I, frankly, I am telling you this frankly, thought it had problems. Basic unfixable problems. In fact, if I had to describe it in a word I would probably describe it as crap."

"I would disagree."

He twinkles, wags his finger, shakes his head, and glides away. I stare after him, relieved and angry, both. Yes there are problems with Iona's book. There is a repetitive quality to some of the scenes and the beginning is overwritten and there is a padded feel to the last three chapters. But she can tell a story better than anyone I've ever read. She can write rings around you, James, I think. And? Rings around me? I look across the room at Iona. She is talking to a famous newspaper columnist; the columnist is smiling, Iona is smiling, all the people around them are smiling as well. She has, I think suddenly, a very fake smile. Professionally fake, like a newscaster's or a politician's. Her teeth are large and sharp and look to me, even from this distance, newly capped. And what was it Joelle said last week? That she thinks Iona may have had her dimples "done" by a plastic surgeon? Nancy says that is why there are no early photos of Iona, and for the first time I am ready to believe this, delighted to believe this. Then Iona beckons and I flinch with quick shame. I make my way across the room, past guests still murmuring, "Deserve it, nice, what she went through," and am introduced to the columnist, who admires the T-shirt and asks me to spell my last name. In the middle of the sixth letter, Iona is pulled away and the columnist pivots and pads after her. I end up standing by Iona's brother who is holding his infant son against his shoulder. His wife comes up to us. "I was talking to someone in the other room?" she says. "And they never even heard about the book?" She looks around, radiant and cross. "They thought this was just a party?"

People are starting to pair up. I see Nancy talking to the piano player and remember her last two boyfriends were musicians. Joelle is talking to a magazine editor about an idea she's had for years. Another editor smiles boldly at me, but I know what he wants; he wants me to interview Iona for him. I've already told him no three times. "I know her too well," I've said. Which is not exactly true. I turn toward a circle of loud laughers, but they are not people I know well either, just faces I've seen on dust jackets over the years. How did Iona meet so many writers so fast? We all started together, Iona and Nancy and Joelle and I, in the same weekend workshop. Now the famous novelist who taught that workshop is here with his famous lover and neither of them seem to see anyone else in the room but Iona. I am shaken by another surge of dislike as I hear the novelist call her his "little star." He didn't even notice Iona in that workshop; she was too quiet; it took Joelle and Nancy and me to notice her, to coax her into taking her strange unfinished story a step further, then another. We are the ones who helped her, who made her a *star*. I steady myself on the back of an old velvet armchair and suddenly remember the sweet sense of peace and pleasure that came over all of us the night Iona sat in this chair and read her revised version to us. The story felt so right, each word the right word, each choice and change completely correct. We listened, Joelle and I side by side on the couch, Nancy lying on her back on the floor, and we knew that something beautiful was happening, and we grinned at each other because we were so glad to be there, and grateful. Send it out, we said to Iona. Share it.

Beside me, someone says, "Is that her real name? Iona?" and someone else, in a lower voice, says, "Sure: I-own-a Jaguar. I-own-a condo." I sigh. Time to go. People are gathering coats and then in one sudden determined exodus they are all heading toward the door. I have the panicky feeling I've had so often lately, of being left behind. Dean and Benjamin are helping the caterers clear. Iona's mother is drifting down the back stairs with her tour guide. James is giving the publicist his card, and KayBeth is striding from room to room asking, "Where is Iona?"

Where is Iona? No one can find her. "Iona? Iona?" people call. "She's on the phone," someone says at last. "She's on the phone to Rio."

And she is still on the phone after I finally find my own coat kicked under the guest room bed with Hissyfit snarling on top of it. I move down the emptying hallway and glance into the study, and there Iona sits, the phone pressed to her ear, her knees drawn up. Joelle and Nancy are also waiting to say good-bye and the three of us crowd in a semicircle, shoulder to shoulder, outside the door. Perched on the stool by her writing desk, Iona looks like a child, like the little girl ghost who never spoke. Nor is she speaking now. Head tipped, neck bent, not seeing us, she rocks, intent. "Who do you suppose she's talking to?" Joelle whispers, and Nancy whispers back, "Her guardian angel," and we giggle, wicked, but just then Iona looks up, and we stop, for her eyes amaze us, they are so light, so full of light, hot and pure and empty and desolate, and Joelle says, strangely, "Don't be afraid," and Nancy says, "We love you," and I say, "It's going to be all right," and we all want to touch her somehow and assure her that her flight into the sun will be long and strong and full of joy—but whether it's because the shiny wings of her dress shift slightly and rise as we watch, or whether because there seems no place on that sleek neat head that can be touched without muss or damage, or because, simply because, we doubt our right to bless at all—for whatever reason our hands drop into weak half-waves, and Joelle and Nancy and I leave Iona there, listening to voices we can't hear.

Creek Walk

SHE COULD NOT WAIT to start cleaning. She drove up to the house the day after her mother's death and began to empty the closets. Wool suits, plaid skirts, silk dresses with bows—everything wearable went into boxes. Handfuls of limp white underwear, bags of old nylons—those she threw out. Her father watched from the doorway, smoking. Some widowers, he told Ann, keep it all. "What for?" he asked her. Ann shook her head. She didn't know. Her father took his bourbon, his cigarettes, and a legal pad into the living room; he was making a list of everyone who phoned. "It was peaceful," she heard him say on the phone. "A coma. No pain."

No pain? Ann glanced at the bed where her mother had died. She had stripped the sheets yesterday and turned the mattress herself. But she could still see Lila's face propped on the pillows that were no longer there. She would always remember the damp skin, the lips pulled back in a snarl for breath, the single tear that pooled and spilled from the unblinking eye. "Mama," she said. She went back to work. She folded scarf upon scarf, linked shoes together. When the bedroom was emptied she began on the bathroom. The medicines first—the hated bottles and vials and tubes and syringes. Next the cosmetics—the lipsticks, face creams, the crystal bottles of darkened perfumes. Efficiently, blindly, Ann swept the clutter into plastic bags, tied the bags together, and set them out for the garbage. She scrubbed the counters and sinks, unwrapped a new soap, a new toothbrush, and hung one fresh towel on every rack. When she was through, her father's few, dull, useful items stood on the tiles like a still life arrangement.

It was raining by the time she left, a spring rain, sparse but persistent. She loaded the boxes of Lila's good clothes on the back of her husband's pickup truck and drove down the hill in a hurry, hoping to get to the thrift shop at the edge of town before it closed for the day. The building was locked when she arrived, but a drop-in bin to one side was propped open. Ann hesitated. She didn't want to leave the clothes there, alone and un-guarded, but the thought of taking them home—keeping them—filled her with horror. The rain fell faster and faster, and finally she opened the door and slid out of the truck. She reached for a box, carried it to the bin, and tipped it in. The whir of soft stuff, unraveling, made her wince. She emptied another box, and another, her face averted. As she went for the last carton, she saw something drop, leap in the wind, and begin to bounce across the vacant parking lot. It was a beige bra, heavily padded. She ran and snatched it up, pressing it close to her body, hiding it within her crossed arms. She was glad she was alone in the lot, glad there was no one to mock her, pro-tecting her mother. She threw the bra into the corroded metal mouth of the bin, dropped the lid with a thud, and ran back through the rain to the truck. "I'm sorry," she said, as she turned the key, shivering. "I'm so sorry, Mama."

It took her another half hour to reach home. The porch light was on, illuminating the path through the overgrown garden. She stopped to pull some weeds sprouting through the mint by the mailbox, and scraped a flake of peeling paint off the porch steps with the side of her boot. Her husband and son were waiting, playing checkers in front of the woodstove. They both looked straight up at her when she entered, into her eyes, as if they could see there what she'd been through that day.

"I brought you some treasures," she said. She tried to sound gay. She unpacked the odds and ends she'd salvaged from Lila's closets. A sealskin cap for Andy to play in. A suede vest she could cut into elbow patches for Jim's flannel shirts. There were two pads of art paper, a set of pastels, a collection of foreign coins, a cowbell, a gold pen and pencil set. There was a mink coat, and—her father had pushed it into her jacket pocket when she left—a brocade pouch of jewels.

"What will you do with all that?" Jim asked. He looked so perplexed that Ann had to smile. Mink and diamonds for a carpenter's wife? They rarely went out. Her job at the library was so casual she could show up in blue jeans and sandals.

"It gets cold in the winter," she reminded him. "And the jewels..." She paused. She didn't yet know what she'd do with the jewels. She hadn't even looked through the pouch yet, not really. She had peeked in once or twice, while she was driving, to make sure the topaz ring was there—it was—and the pearls—they were there too. Now she smoothed the mink coat against her body, wrapped it in a plastic bag, and went to put it away in the hall closet. The shelves of the closet were inexplicably jammed. There were piles of overalls Andy had outgrown years ago, stacks of flowered sheets faded by line drying, worn bath mats and towels. She began sorting and folding. She was startled to look up and see Jim, naked, blinking in the doorway. "It's after midnight, babe," he said. "What are you doing?"

Doing? Grieving. She was too old to cry—or too cold—something. Tears shot out in tiny spurts, usually when she was in the shower. She would cry "Mama" and reach out, choking, for a towel to press to her eyes. But the fit passed in seconds. There was no long bout of weeping—if she lay down on the bed to cry she soon fell asleep. She slept all the time. She went to bed as soon as the dishes were done and she lay without moving until morning. She napped on the couch in the library's lunch room. On her day off she drove Andy to school, came home, and crawled straight into his narrow, gritty bed, where she dozed all day. "What's the matter?" Jim asked, when he came home and found her kneeling, in her kimono, in Andy's room, sorting comic books into piles.

"I don't know," Ann said. "I just don't feel good."

"What do you feel like?"

Well, she felt as if she had a low-grade fever or an ongoing hangover. She couldn't move quickly; she couldn't hear very well. It was a lot of trouble to talk. She felt bruised inside and had, in fact, somehow managed to acquire real black-and-blue marks on her thighs and arms—she could not remember how. Her fingernails fascinated her; she studied them all the time; they did not seem to be growing and looked ridged and thin. She had stopped going to her aerobics class at the high school; she did not suppose she would ever go again. The idea of bouncing around to loud music was very distasteful. She wanted to cook but could not seem to manage to get to the store, or find the right items when she did; she opened cans of tuna or beans and found herself absently, methodically, finishing everything Andy left on his plate. She could tell she was gaining weight; the waistband on the skirt she had been wearing for the last four days was starting to pinch. She felt bloated and weak.

"I think you should see a doctor," Jim said. "I think it's your thyroid."

"It's not my thyroid. It's...you know." She did not want to say the word *grief*. She looked up at Jim. He had been working outside; his broad face was sunburned. The baseball cap Lila had bought him—the one that said "Einstein"—perched on top of his curls.

"I hate that hat," she said.

"What for? It's a great hat." He touched the rim and grinned down at her. She dropped her eyes and studied the comic books. She had sorted them into piles by hero. Now it was time to put them into chronological order.

"I'll buy you a new one," she offered.

"With what? Our inheritance?"

"*My* inheritance."

She let out her breath, instantly sorry. Lila had once told her that Jim was the worst man she could marry—he was too simple, Lila had said, too slow, too unambitious. But even Lila had known, toward the end, she was wrong. Lila had relied on Jim's strong arms to carry her from her bed to her couch in the living room; she had relied on his sweetness, his humor, his calm. When Ann looked up and saw Jim examining the cap in his huge hands, unperturbed, she smiled. Jim did not smile back. "I just don't want you to get sick," he said seriously.

"I won't," she assured him. "I'm not like my mother."

Lila had been sick for years. Even before the cancer was diagnosed, the little mirrored tray by Lila's bed had been crowded with pills. She had had diabetes, hypertension, rheumatoid arthritis, colitis. She had broken her back, her neck, her big toe, her elbow. She would recover from one ailment only to come down with another. Part of it, the doctors said, was her own fault. She would not relax; she would not take it easy. She had always been a perfectionist, restless, dissatisfied. "The hard way is the right way," she used to repeat when Ann, as a child, balked at repetitive homework assignments or piano practice. Ann remembered that voice—so brisk, so complacent, so grim. She remembered the way Lila threw herself into dancing, gardening, golfing, Italian lessons, oil painting. She could see her mother canning peaches in the kitchen on a hot afternoon, her hair frizzed with sweat; she could see her straining at a ballet bar or frowning over an intricate piece of needlework.

"She had a hard life," Ann said, trying to explain Lila to Andy. Andy listened, expressionless. Lila's last sentence to him had been, "Don't kiss me until you've washed your face," and he had backed away from her bedside, silent. "She couldn't help the way she was," Ann continued. "She loved you." She put her arm around Andy and held him as close as he'd let her. That was the good part—if there was a good part—to the last months of dying: the love. Lila had softened toward others, and Ann, at last, had softened toward Lila. She had liked Lila, finally. She had admired her courage, pitied her intolerance, enjoyed her gossip and boastings. It had been fun, dropping by after work to sit by Lila's bed. She had opened windows, shut them, rearranged the white roses in the silver vase, wiped the smudges off the mirror, adjusted the paintings. She had done whatever Lila asked, and, for once, without resentment. The hours spent reading out loud, watching talk shows on television, gently shampooing and combing Lila's fine blond hair, had been among the happiest in her life.

But, she thought, I did want her to die.

They all had. Her father, her brother, the nurse—they had all been appalled by the last days of pain. "Lila, it's time," they had said. "There's a time to hold on and a time to let go." And Lila had said, "But I don't want to let go." Lila had died with tears in her eyes.

Mama, Ann thought. She remembered how happy they'd all felt, when Lila stopped breathing. How still and peaceful the world felt, without her. When the doctor arrived they'd poured brandy and joked and he had joked back, as if their behavior was natural, as if horror and helplessness were as common as colds, to be cured with sweet wine. And the wine worked for a while; it helped. Other things had helped since—the calls from old friends, the boxes of photos she and her brother had spent an afternoon going through, the jewels. Ann knew it was shameful, but she had to admit it: the jewels helped a lot.

The jewels lay jumbled in the brocade pouch and Ann moved the pouch almost every day, looking for the safest hiding place. Inside a teapot, on the shelf with the Christmas ornaments, wrapped up in a sleeping bag. Often she awoke with her heart pounding, afraid she'd mislaid them. Once she got up and tried them all on—the rope of pearls, the diamond earrings, the three watches, the bracelets—she rested her chin on the collar of the fur coat and turned back and forth before the hall mirror. Her lips were somber but her eyes were alight. She had wanted these things all her life. She had counted on having them, had looked forward for years. She had found herself staring at a gold bracelet, a jade pendant, fixing on it, helpless to look away even when Lila was alive and talking to her. Now they were hers and she was glad to have them. It was most peculiar and exciting to stand there in bare feet and finery while her son and husband slept; she felt like an actress, she felt like a thief. It was a long while before she finally slipped off the fur and put the jewels back in the pouch. Some, she knew, she would sell. They had already begun to mean less to her, and Jim would be glad for the money. But the topaz ring she would never sell. The topaz ring would stay on her right hand forever. She dropped the pouch into one of Jim's old ski boots and began to align all the shoes on the closet floor in rows. The ring winked and twinkled as she worked.

It was not an expensive ring—the jeweler she took it to for appraisal was mildly contemptuous—nor did it look good on Ann's hand, which, with its pinkish skin and blunt squared nails, resembled her father's. But it had been Lila's engagement ring and something of Lila's—her defiance maybe—seemed to Ann to reside inside the stone. The ring, in a way Ann did not wish to explain, *was* Lila. She found herself straightening it again and again, as if it were a small eye that needed to be refocused. She wanted to show it the best parts of her world—the hard green plums on the tree near the creek that had, until this year, always been barren; Andy racing across the fields with his kite; Jim's face above her as they made Sunday morning love.

She was wearing the topaz, and the diamond earrings, and the jade pendant one afternoon when she saw her father at a shopping mall. He was so close behind another couple that she thought they might all be together; he was trailing them as the third always does, as she herself had done following her parents through crowds. Only when the other couple disappeared into a shop did she see he was alone. She crossed over, tapped him on the shoulder, and said, "Hey handsome." He turned, unsurprised, a tall old man in a yellowish suit. He said, "What are you doing here?" and she felt herself flush. She was shopping for a bathing suit. There was nothing wrong with that. She needed a bathing suit. "What are *you* doing here?" she countered. They stared at each other, astonished, then Ann touched his arm. "Why don't you come for dinner tonight?"

"Just came yesterday."

"Come again."

He did. He didn't seem to mind the long drive; he said it relaxed him. He didn't seem to think Jim was too dull, or Andy too noisy, or the house too disheveled. He sat in the kitchen and ate everything she fed him—the tacos seasoned with a mix, the frozen cake. He smoked incessantly and showed her his lists—the lists of those who had written, phoned, sent flowers or food. "Everyone seems to think I ought to be relieved," he said, tapping his cigarette out, his fingers already reaching for another. He raised his bourbon glass, his pale eyes on Ann. "I don't feel relieved. I feel..."

Desolate, Ann thought. Bereaved. Bereft. Alone. "It's harder for you," she began. "As a husband, I mean." She couldn't finish her thought. But it seemed to her that for most of his life her father had been struggling to capture the same woman she had been struggling to escape. She had a daughter's history of resistance that he, as a husband, lacked. He had not just learned to like Lila; he had always liked her. When she was outrageous, he laughed; when she was moody, he ignored her; when she was thin and pale and wasting away, he had raised her hand to his lips and kissed it. Ann had observed her father's responses to her mother all her life, and she had never understood them. He seemed to be wooing a stranger. Ann thought how she'd feel if she lost Jim: hollowed out. If Andy died she would want to die herself. But losing Lila was not that important. After a certain age, no one needed a mother. "You must feel so much worse than I," she finished lamely. She looked down at the kitchen floor, which was dull and discolored.

"I don't know about that," her father said. "I just know I don't feel *relieved.*" He accepted the cup of black coffee Jim poured him and began to show Andy how to draw horses. It was nice, Ann realized, having him here without Lila. It was good to have him all to herself. The thought was so primitive—so satisfying—that she smiled. Her father, looking up, smiled shyly back. Ann walked him to his car, her arm around his waist. After he drove away she came back in and studied the kitchen floor. It was stained in places, and would probably need to be stripped with a wire brush and re-waxed.

"I'm not worried about Mom's soul," her brother said. "She's in good hands. You can't beat God's hands."

"You sound like a sportscaster," Ann said. She arranged the spices in alphabetical order as she held the kitchen phone to her ear. Tom had called her three times this last week. He was upset that their father still refused to have a church service for Lila.

"Joke if you want to," Tom said, "but it's you I'm worried about. You, Dad, her friends. You're the ones who need it. It doesn't matter to Mom. She's in her heavenly home."

"Andy thinks she's up in the sky watching us," Ann said. "He thinks if he forgets to brush his teeth, Grandma's going to reach down from the ceiling and get him." She laughed; Tom did not.

"I really don't understand your resistance to some simple communal prayers," Tom said.

Ann said nothing. She remembered the way Tom had stood at the end of Lila's bed and read from the Bible in a deep strong voice. She respected his faith. Perhaps she even envied it. But it wasn't for her. She slid the cumin next to the curry. "You'll just have to pray for all of us," she told him.

"I do," Tom assured her. "I have been."

After he hung up, she centered the cinnamon and looked out the window. She could see Jim, through the kitchen window, sweeping the deck, and Andy, disconsolate, trailing behind him. She had been so busy with housework lately she had not spent much time with Andy. She opened the back door. "Want to do something?" she called.

"There's nothing to do," he answered.

"Nothing to do?" Ann spread her arms out. It was a warm spring Sunday. A few clouds drifted across a soft blue sky; the creek behind their house sparkled and splashed. "We live in one of the most beautiful places in the world," she said, "and you have nothing to do?"

"I wanted to go exploring," Andy said, "but Dad won't go with me."

"Why can't you go by yourself?"

Andy shrugged and banged a stick on the deck rail. "Let's do this," Ann suggested. "Let's explore the creek. We'll take a litter bag and clean up as we go."

The creek was the clear brown of weak coffee. A few yellow leaves— where had they come from?—floated at the edges of the deep pools and gathered between the rocks in the shallows. "Look at the junk," Ann whistled. There were plastic bottles and beer cans and strange long strips of Saran Wrap. They followed the creek as it wound behind their house, flowed under a footbridge, edged through a ravine. Ann balanced from rock to rock in her tennis shoes, the litter bag over her back; Andy followed. When she raised her eyes she saw steep banks of blackberry rising on either side of them. It was very quiet. Insects whirred in the sunlight, water scooters sped before them, there was a dank spicy scent of wet rocks and mud.

"How far does it go?" Ann asked.

"I don't know," Andy said. "I've never been this far before."

"Let's follow it out to the ocean," Ann said.

"Mom. That would take days."

"I want to see where it goes though, don't you?" She picked up a piece of torn cloth and a strand of green string. Part of a barbecue grate lay caught in the roots of an overhanging laurel tree. As she tugged it free she felt her foot slipping. Oh, no, she thought. She turned to look at Andy, who was grinning at her. "Help!" she clowned, and then she fell backward into a pool, where she sank in cold water up to her knees. She sloshed toward the bank. Something dark darted toward her—a fish? a *fish?*—and she screamed with real fright. She climbed onto the bank, her arms full of garbage, laughing. I can't be laughing, she thought, my mother just died. She touched the ring, to make sure it was safe. Andy started toward her, deliberately lost his footing, and fell in too. After that they didn't bother staying on the rocks, but waded down the center of the creek, splashing loudly.

She met her friend Nadia for lunch the next week. She told her about the creek walk and how strange she and Andy had felt when they crawled up the ravine only to emerge, scratched and triumphant, less than a mile from their house. "We were gone for hours," she explained. "We really thought we were getting somewhere."

Nadia nodded, listening. She was older than Ann, with a husband almost as old as Ann's father. Ann always felt she could tell Nadia anything—any secret, any dream, any minor, shameful complaint—but today, for some reason, she found all she wanted to talk about, after she'd talked about the creek, was food and music and movie stars, and Nadia, too, seemed content with such small talk. She examined Ann's fingernails and recommended gelatin; she wrote down the name of a new frozen yogurt store in town. They both laughed often, sighed often, paused. When they left the restaurant, Ann leaned toward Nadia and kissed her on the lips. She didn't know why. She had never kissed a woman friend on the lips before. The taste was sweet and dry and it made an impression that lasted all day. She touched her own lips. She thought the word *Mama*.

Mama. Who was Mama? Lila wasn't Mama. Lila was a tall blond in glasses. Lila spoke baby talk to animals, craved lemons, cried in the bathroom. Lila had set her easel up in the museum under a Cézanne and copied it, stroke by stroke, four times, slashing each canvas, when it was finished, with a straight-edged razor. Lila knew two Beethoven sonatas by heart and played them at parties; when she missed a note she banged her fist on the keyboard, took a deep breath, and began over again. Lila's last words had been, "I am so frustrated," and Lila had died.

Mama hadn't. Mama had just gone away. Mama wasn't Lila or Mommy or Mom or Mother. Mama was far more elusive. A small hole in a white space no one could stitch up, a gap at heart's center. Mama belonged here, beside Ann, behind Ann—inside Ann—but Ann couldn't find her. She was not in the mirror, behind the curtains, in the car, on the telephone. She was not in the sunset, the soccer field, the supermarket—she was not and she would not be and Ann knew this and Ann could not understand this. Ann stood with her hands out, impatient and forlorn, wanting her Mama.

One night she sat at the desk Jim had built for her and began to write a letter. She was very tired, a little high. "Dear Mama," she wrote. She paused and looked out the open window into the moonlit garden. She was remembering her last morning with Lila, the morning when she should have said, "I love you," the morning when she should have said, "good-bye." If the nurse had left us alone, she thought. If the oxygen tank had not been so loud. She remembered Lila's face, alert and fierce and swollen, and her bare slight body under the sheets. There had been something she'd wanted to say to her then, something she wanted to say to her now. "You are beautiful," she wrote. "You always were beautiful to me and you always will be. You are the person who taught me what beauty is. You taught me what to look for in the world. What to honor. What to fight for. What to keep." She put the pen down. The garden blurred through her rush of brief tears, and she felt herself spinning in a world of shadows and spangles and owl calls and the scent of night jasmine. This was your world once, she thought. Mine now. Andy's later. Nothing lasts. Thank you.

"Everyone hold hands," Tom ordered. Ann took one of Mona Thompson's hands and one of Elsie Biggs's. Jim was at the far end of the circle, between Andy and the hospice nurse. The sun fell through the high windows of the living room of her father's house, gilding everyone's hair, making the champagne glasses waiting on the bar counter glitter. Pastor Neilsen bent his healthy handsome head and began to pray. Ann listened as hard as she could, but at his first mistake—he called Lila "Ada"—her thoughts drifted away. She wondered when Howard Bently had begun to wear a hearing aid— what was Mildred doing on crutches—had Elsie always quaked like this? How old her mother's friends had become, and how quickly! She was relieved when the pastor finally stopped praying but looked up in horror when Tom began to sing. A thrill of shame shot through her and she glanced toward her father, but her father was studying the carpet and seemed lost in thought. Tom's voice was loud and tuneless and the hymn he was singing sounded like something he'd just made up. Ann stared at him furiously, willing him to stop. But something in the way he stood, with his hands clenched, and his eyes on the distance, and his strong young chin jutting out, made her close her eyes at last. He's just like Mama, she thought. He looks more like Mama than I do, and he has more to say to her, and he's saying it his own way, and I have to let him. She sang "Amen" with the others, took a deep breath, and thought: Well, that's over.

But it wasn't. Her father called her late the next week. She had been sleeping. "There's a drawer you forgot," he said.

"A drawer?" She was too sleepy to know what he was talking about.

"I went to open a drawer and it was full of her things." He was speaking in an alert, quick voice; he sounded sober and young.

"I'll come tomorrow and empty it," she promised. She went back to bed and wondered what was in the drawer—diaries, perhaps, or pain pills. She slept and dreamed the drawer was full of fish, living fish, with cold tears slipping from their silver eyes. She awoke and lay still, staring up at the ceiling. Jim, beside her, woke too.

"What's the matter, babe?" he murmured.

"Just a dream," she told him. The fish were all different sizes and they needed to be sorted and separated. Some went to the ocean, some to the creek, some to a lake in the mountains she'd never seen. She reached for Jim's hand. "I'll never get it all done," she said, and then she fell asleep again.

Maximum Security

I DIDN'T GET THE PROMOTION. I found out yesterday; Dieter called to tell me at home. Dieter is semiretired from the firm, but as senior vice president he knows everyone and hears everything, and he is often asked to mediate between the officers and the rest of us. "They gave it," he said, his voice subdued and melodic, "to Lenora Press."

"Lenora Press?" I had to think. "Oh, yes. I know her. We worked on a project together last year. She's nice. But"—I had to say it—"she's twenty-five years old."

"Twenty-four," Dieter said.

We were both silent. Dieter is sixty-seven and I am forty-two. I felt every year of both our ages, plus a few extra, as I stood there holding the phone. I felt thick and shorter than I am, and rumpled, as if all my clothes needed to be washed, starched, and reironed. I noted that the bare wood floor needed to be swept again, and that all the prints on the wall were crooked.

"They reason," said Dieter, "that since she's so young, she'll stay with the firm a long time."

"And I won't?" My mind continued its moody math: forty-two minus death age still equaled "a long time"—didn't it? Maybe it didn't. I shifted the phone to my other ear.

"They seem to think," Dieter continued, "that she'll grow with the firm."

"Do what?" When I'm under stress I get stupid and hear things the way children or foreigners do. "Grow with the firm" was suddenly a new set of words that made no sense at all. I narrowed my eyes and tried to imagine Lenora Press stretched to the size of our building downtown.

"You know," Dieter prompted. "Expand with the company."

Now I saw her ballooning up, buoyant with computer printouts, memos, metal desks, and software. I shook my head, to clear it. "What a fate," I said.

Dieter laughed, relieved I had my sense of humor back. I of course no longer knew what a sense of humor was. Lenora Press was a tall, quiet freckled girl who wore her hair parted down the middle with two barrettes to hold it back. She was allergic to house dust, fur, and pollen, carried a photo of a niece in her wallet, lived alone, and drove a dark, shiny, late-model German sedan. I only wanted this promotion, I protested rapid-fire to myself, because, unlike Lenora Press, I had other people to worry about: I had three children and an ex-husband to support. It's not just the money, I reminded myself. It's the benefits. With the new dental insurance I'd hoped to get braces for the kids and bridgework for myself. What would Lenora Press do with free dental insurance? Her teeth were perfect, short and milky. I sucked a cracked molar and pushed back a grey hair.

"You know what I think happened?" Dieter's voice dropped, became fruity. He was going to console me with compliments. "I think they just decided to play it safe. You've always been too good for this firm. Too free. You know? Too sassy."

Ah ha, I thought. That's what happened. At some point I wasn't respectful enough. I stepped on some toes. I spoke up when I should have been silent, laughed at the wrong time, hurt someone's feelings. But whose—and when—and where? I wanted Dieter to tell me what I'd done wrong, when I'd been sassy, so I could fix it, and make sure it never happened again.

"You could get a job anywhere," Dieter said.

I opened my mouth but did not cut him off. I liked being told that. I felt like a house cat who is being cooed to even as it's being dropped out the back door at bedtime. I'll look for an executive position in Paris, I thought. I'll see what's open in the South Pacific. I'll show her, I thought, and then I thought: no. Calm down. This has nothing to do with Lenora Press. She's a quiet, decent, hardworking, intelligent, and resourceful—child—but it's not her fault. It's not even their fault, the officers. I thought of the three men who had interviewed me for the promotion. One was a closet gay and one was an alcoholic and one was an old-fashioned skirt chaser. They were all depressed, and out of shape, and facing retirement, and I wouldn't want to be them, or be like them, and it probably showed. That's what happened. It probably showed.

After Dieter hung up I straightened all the prints in the hallway and then I went into the kitchen to get the broom and sweep off the floor. As I passed the kids' room I called in, "Well, guess what. I didn't get the promotion."

"Don't worry, I'll support you," my oldest son said.

"I will," my youngest son said.

"You can't, you're a doo-doo."

"I'm not a doo-doo, you're a dodo."

My daughter followed me into the kitchen and when I bent into the broom closet she put her arms around my waist and hugged me. "Poor poor Mom," she said.

"Thank you," I said, "and please tell the boys to knock it off."

I patted her, the way you do when you want someone to let go of you, and after a second she lifted her head and gave me one of those long, full, tragic looks she's picked up from television sitcom shows.

"Everything's going to be all right," I reminded her. "We don't have to sell your stuffed animals. I still have my old job."

"Just not the job you wanted," she said.

"No one has the job they want."

I picked up the broom and swept out the hall and half of the living room. Dirt shows more now since Sven took the rugs and sold them. He's promised as soon as he's back on his feet he'll buy us some more, but we've all become used to the bare hardwood floor. The boys take beach towels and scoot from corner to corner, pretending they're surfers, and my daughter likes to sit cross-legged in the center and play jacks. I studied the contents of the dustpan—sand, cat hair, crayon chips, one small, nimble spider—enough stuff to send Lenora Press to the hospital for a week if I could figure out a way to smuggle it into her car; no, I thought, for the second time that morning, no and no and no. I carried the dustpan outside to dump.

It was a beautiful morning in early April. The lilac tree I planted ten years ago was in bloom against the garage, and a mockingbird called from a neighbor's roof. I sat down on the back porch and cried a little—but only a little, for one of the things about being forty-two is that your tear ducts dry up, and you can't cry a lot. I heard a car pull up in front—the baby-sitter can drive herself over now, she's sixteen already; she'll be twenty-four soon, wanting my job. I could feel the crow's-feet with my fingertips as I pushed the tears back, and, yes, high on one cheek, a brand new pimple coming in. Middle-age acne. The worst of both worlds.

I stood up. It was the day for my women's group meeting. We are all professional women—I like the sound of that phrase, as if there are amateur women who can't get their sex organs attached in the morning—and we meet once a month to complain and explain and just be with each other. I brushed off my jeans and picked up my shoulder bag on my way out the front door. From the way the children had positioned themselves around the baby-sitter, arms linked like some stricken frontier family, I knew they had told her. "Have fun," they called sadly.

"I will," I assured them. I got into the car. Maybe it was the Resist Authority sticker on the bumper that lost me the promotion. Maybe it was the cold french fries wedged into the cracks of the passenger seat. Maybe it was the mockingbird mess on the windshield.

Or maybe it was the way I drove, for I drove like an idiot, almost rear-ending a pickup truck before I remembered another favorite phrase: Slow Down Stupid. I took my foot off the gas, lifted my head, and took a deep breath. The meeting was at Annie's house, which is a block away from one of the most expensive clothing stores in town. I deliberately forced myself not to look into the windows as I passed, but it did no good, for Annie was dressed in new leather pants from that store, and a new silk blouse, and was pouring champagne as I came in. "We're celebrating," she explained. "I signed my new contract yesterday."

"Well congratulations," I said.

"And what happened with you and your promotion?" She smiled and held out a glass of champagne.

"Oh." I shrugged. "I didn't get it. They gave it to Lenora Press."

"I know Lenora Press." Barbara came in and sat down at the kitchen table beside me. "She used to be with Minto and Chambers. She's...young."

"Yeah," I said.

"Real, real young," Barbara said.

"I don't like her name," said Patricia. "Lenora. It sounds like someone's grandmother's name."

"Watch what you say about grandmothers," Tanya warned, "or I'll make you look at my photos again." No one laughed—Tanya has about a hundred photos of her grandson that she keeps in her briefcase, so, after dunking her butter cookie into her coffee, Tanya said, "I see this is serious. OK. Let's have a cheering up session. I'll start. Yesterday I was downtown and I stepped off the curb to my car and I fell. It was two o'clock in the afternoon, I was dead sober, as always, and I had on my Anne Klein suit, you know the one, with the piping down the front. I sprained my foot. I couldn't get up. And you know what happened? Nothing. People just kept walking past me. Hundreds of people on the sidewalk, all in a hurry, all walking past me. One man finally did stop. He looked a minute and sort of nodded to himself and walked on. I think he'd decided I was changing the oil under my car."

We all stared at Tanya, who never has a hair out of place, wears bright red lipstick, and is a lawyer for one of the biggest firms in the country. "What did you do?" we asked.

"I dragged myself up and drove to the hospital. Look." She lifted a foot, which was bandaged. "That was the easy part. The hard part was realizing that all at once and for no good reason I was invisible."

"Sometimes," Patricia said, "it's good to be invisible. I was standing outside my building at lunchtime—it was my birthday?—and this old man walked up to me and said,' " You know what you are? You are the devil incarnate.' "

Once again we stared. Patricia is a round-faced blond with dimples and the rosiest cheeks I've ever seen on an adult; even with horns and a tail she'd look like a cherub.

"He must have been crazy," Annie said for all of us. "What did you say to him?"

"What could I say?" Patricia said. "Thank you? I didn't say anything."

"I wasn't going to say anything either," Barbara said, after a minute, "but you know that guy I've been seeing—Roger? We drove up the coast last weekend and we stayed at this romantic inn and went out for this great dinner and in the middle of the night he lit a candle and knelt by the side of the bed and said, 'Barbara, I have to ask you something,' and I just lay there holding my breath and he said, 'Can I borrow two hundred thousand dollars?' "

We started to laugh, we couldn't help it. I put my arm around Barbara and she put her arm around Tanya who encircled Patricia who reached for Annie and we sat there, laughing as gently as if we were all bubbling together in one huge pot. Finally Patricia said, "This is some meeting. If it weren't for Annie's good news, I'd suggest we all go out and kill ourselves."

"My news is good," Annie agreed. "But here's something that will fit right in. I've been wanting to get my face lifted, you've all heard me talking about it, and I know I'm obsessed, but I just can't decide. So there's this kid at work. He's just a copy boy but we goof around a lot and the other day I said, 'What do you think? Should I get a face lift?' And he looked at me a long time and then he said, 'No.' And I thought, Good! He thinks I don't need one! And then he said, 'Why go through all that pain when you don't have much time left?' "

It's not funny, I thought, as I drove home. It's not even comforting. It's like being told, when you're a kid and scared of dying, Don't worry, everyone dies. What good does that do? No one should die, I'd always known that. No one should die and everyone should get exactly what they want. Tanya should be helped off the street by a lawyer as elegant and knowledgeable as she is and they should sue the world. Patricia should have strangers laying flowers at her feet. Barbara should have two hundred thousand dollars to refuse to lend Roger, and Annie's face should be on the cover of every fashion magazine in the country. And I—well—I should be fruitfully employed.

Fruitfully employed is another phrase I like, and I rolled it around on my tongue as I stopped at the supermarket. There were only eight dollars left in my checking account but I bought fresh salmon steaks and new asparagus tips and homemade pasta and raspberries from Peru anyway. It was the sort of Judgment Day shopping that would make my lover, Brad, who is an economist, bolt into a full-fledged lecture. But Brad would never know—he was gone for the weekend, camping with his own kids. I missed him and wished he were in town so I could tell him about my promotion, about not getting it. He'd heard me say nothing for weeks but, "I know I won't get it, I know they won't take me," and he'd always said, "Don't be so negative about yourself. Don't you know your own worth?"

No, I wanted to tell him now. I never have known and neither has anyone else. I sniffled a little. Was Lenora Press "worth" more than I just because she was younger and less sassy? What had Dieter meant by sassy in the first place? I had always been meek, too meek. In the interview with the three officers I had sat straight up in my chair and I had answered each and every question as humbly as a Sunday school prize child. Well. Maybe not every question. I remembered one of the men peering at me over his cigarette, which I had not asked him to put out. "If you could do one thing," he had asked, "to change the firm, what would you do?" And I had laughed uncontrollably and said I'd been with the firm for seven years and no one had been able to change it yet. They'd all looked at each other and said, "Seven years? She's been with us that long?"

Seven years is a long time to stay in a job. After seven years you know who lies to his clients and who keeps a quart of vodka in his desk and whose mother phones four times a week. These officers had no secrets from me, I knew them too well. They could be new, and they could be charming, for Lenora. Poor Lenora, I thought. Still, I dreaded having to go in on Monday and congratulate her. I'd have to smile and be cheerful and act as if I didn't care.

And I did care. It took me a long time to admit it, but I cared a lot. I had a hard time sleeping that night and once or twice I woke up and thought: maybe this whole thing is a dream, maybe Dieter never called me. But I knew he had. Finally, toward morning, I did have a dream. I dreamt I was a man named Max, and when I asked someone why my name was Max they said, "Maximum Security, get it? You need all the security you can get, ha ha," and when I woke up I lay still thinking about that, and wondering what it meant. I'd had a crew cut in the dream—I touched my own hair, to make sure it was still there—and I was wearing prison clothes. Maximum security, get it? No, I thought, and without that promotion I was too poor to pay a psychiatrist to explain it to me.

"Yoo-hoo." Someone rattled the outside of the bedroom window and I opened my eyes again to see Sunday morning flooding in full through the curtains, and a dark stout shadow pacing outside. It was my neighbor, Maria. "You promised to jog with me today and if you're not out in two minutes I'm going to come in and get you," she said.

"I'm coming," I called. "I'm up." I pulled on some sweats and splashed water on my face and said good morning to the kids who were eating toast and oranges on the bare floor in front of cartoons.

"See?" my youngest boy said. "I told you she wasn't depressed."

"I told you," my oldest boy said, and kicked him.

"We thought you were going to stay in bed all day," my daughter explained.

"I've never done that." They all looked at me. "Have I?"

"Once around Christmas," my daughter reminded me.

"And your birthday," the boys said together.

"Those were holidays." I stepped out the front door and blinked at Maria, who looked as bleary as I, with wrinkle cream under her eyes and acne cream on her chin. Maria, who has been married for twenty-one years to a well-fed and contented husband, is the only true man-hater I know. She did not like Sven, especially after he took the rugs, and she thinks even less of Brad—she calls him Brad X. "I believe in marriage," she told me once, "but that's as far as I'll go." She took one look at me as I stood up, dizzy from tying my laces, and shook her head.

"Those bastards," she said. "They didn't give you the promotion after all. Well. Who cares. You can always get another promotion." She adjusted her diamond ring until it was bright enough to blind a passing motorist and began to jog. I let her set the pace and fell in step beside her. It was hard to get started but after a few minutes I could feel my blood start to stir and my cheeks start to burn in the cool morning air. "They're idiots," she said. "I hope they rot. They probably hired some dick from the home office."

"Actually," I said, "they hired a woman."

"Don't say woman when you mean bimbo." I breathed beside her, soothed. "So where is Brad when you need him?"

"He'll be back tomorrow."

"Tomorrow." She nodded. "Mr. On-the-Spot. Mr. Lean-on-Me." She glanced at me sideways. I knew what she was thinking. An Eskimo would know what she was thinking. She was thinking that after two years with Brad I ought to be getting more from him. I ought to be married, or at least promoted." You know your problem?" she said. "Life is hard and you're too soft."

"I am not," I panted.

"Where are your rugs then?"

"Oh, lord." I had to stop and hold my side. "The rugs. Sven was counting on my promotion. Now he'll probably want to sell the piano."

"Screw Sven," Maria said simply. We jogged in amicable silence the rest of the way home. As we came toward the gate I saw that my house looked even smaller and shabbier than usual, with the kids' skateboards in the driveway and weeds poking through the gravel and the For Sale sign on the lawn. With the money from the promotion, I'd hoped to yank that sign up and chop it for firewood. I pulled my eyes away and saw Sven driving up the street. "Speaking of the devil," Maria said, as he parked in front. "What does he do, drop by and take the kids off your hands for half an hour once a month? Mr. Family Man. Where do you find them?"

"Someday," Sven said, after Maria curtsied to him and left, "I'm going to run over your fat little friend."

"She'd puncture your tires with her teeth."

"Yeah, well, with these tires." He shook his head sadly. "These tires are really worn out. I need four new ones. And a new transmission. This whole car is shot."

"Don't tell me about it. I can't help you."

"They didn't give it to you, huh." His hand fell heavy on my shoulder as we entered the house. Inside was cool and dark and cluttered. The children were dressed and ready to go but Sven kept his hand on my shoulder and I felt the weight, as I'd always felt it, as if I were a little pillar and he a huge roof about to cave in. No wonder I sometimes felt cracked. "Well you know what you're like in interviews, hon," he said at last. "You probably said exactly the wrong thing at exactly the wrong time."

I thought about that after he and the children drove off, and I decided, after a while, that he didn't know a dodo from doo-doo; I had never fudged a single interview in the whole time he was married to me, he just said that to make me feel bad, throwing in the "hon" for good measure—and it worked. It's all worked, I thought. Everything everyone, including myself, had done to make me feel bad had worked. Dieter had called me sassy, and I wasn't sassy, and Maria had called me soft, and I wasn't that either. I was...well, at forty-two I didn't know what I was. I was still growing. I wasn't through yet.

I paced around the house, restless as I always am right after the kids leave. I was tempted to plop down on the floor and start playing jacks for the rest of the day, and I was equally tempted to drive straight to the expensive store near Annie's house and charge hundreds of dollars in leather and silks. What should I do, I thought, what should I do? And I realized that what I wanted to do was exactly what I always did on Sundays, so I turned on the radio and blasted some Bach, and made some fresh coffee and picked my pimple and did some dishes and sorted some laundry and paid some bills and knitted a few rows on the sweater I'm making for Brad's birthday, and then I took a plate of cold salmon and raspberries out to the picnic table by the lilac tree and sat down in the sun with the want ads, and all the time I was repeating, I didn't get the promotion, I didn't get the promotion, waiting for the words to stop sounding foreign and form a known, familiar phrase, a phrase as plain as a wooden plank, solid enough to stand on, once I was ready to stand, strong enough to walk on, once I knew where to go.

Survival in the Wilderness

THE MINUTE HENRY LEFT the house, Sherry began to go through his things. She knew it was wrong. She knew if Henry walked back in and found her naked on her hands and knees peering under his mattress she'd die. What could she say? Oh, hi, honey, I just lost an earring. That wouldn't work. Henry was too observant for that. He'd see at once that both her earrings were firmly affixed to both burning ears. He'd see she was lying. He'd see she was spying. He'd see that the girl he thought he'd left sweetly asleep in his bed—the girl he thought was so "nice" and "bright" and "funny"— was not the real girl at all, but a fake.

And then he'd break off with her. Because Henry believed in trust. Without trust, Henry often said, there is nothing. And Sherry agreed. She had no trust and she often felt nothing. She slid down on her belly and groped under the bed. Oh, hi, hon, she would say, if he burst back through the door. Just looking for something to read. Like your diary.

If Henry kept a diary, though, he didn't keep it under his bed. Sherry struggled up, rocked back on her heels, and studied the stash she'd retrieved: a hiking boot, a compass, a vitamin C pill, and a handful of grey flattened popcorn. She frowned at the popcorn. Would a man, by himself, eat popcorn in bed? Henry had never eaten popcorn in bed with her; did this mean, as she feared, he was seeing someone else? She only knew what he told her. He'd told her he was a simple man with simple tastes who had "strong feelings" for her but liked "doing things"—camping, hiking, sailing—on his own, and that sounded fine, on the surface, but they had been together eight months and it seemed to Sherry that the list of "things" had grown, while the "feelings" had not.

It was time to take stock. Sherry tucked her hair behind her ears, shoved the popcorn back under the bed, and stood up. She didn't have much time—Henry had gone to the city to pick up his son and he'd be back in an hour. She had never been alone in his house before; she'd have to move fast. There were backpacks to go through, address books to read, that lavender letter she'd seen lying on top of his desk last night. She pulled on a pair of jeans, plucked one of Henry's plaid flannel shirts off the back of a chair, and buttoned it quickly over her bare skin. It smelled good, like Henry. It felt like Henry hugging her, not that Henry would be hugging her, if he knew what she was doing.

And what was she doing? Nothing, really. Exploring a bit. The same thing Henry told her he was doing when he took off alone with his skis or his kayak. Scouting the territory. Getting a feel for the lay of the land. The old show tune "Getting to Know You" began to whistle softly through Sherry's teeth. She rolled up her sleeves, put on a pair of thick glasses she kept hidden in a pocket of her purse, and set to work.

Henry's house was like Henry himself, dark and rough and riddled with secrets. It was an old hunting lodge in the hills outside the city, high-beamed, small-windowed, built with deep wooden cupboards and window seats that opened. There was a trap door leading down to the basement and a false brick in the fireplace. Henry had made a great show of opening it up for her once. "See," he had said, "I've got nothing to hide." The grimy little crypt had been empty that time but when Sherry reached in this morning the first thing she felt was a knife. A Swiss Army knife, a bullet case, a GI Joe doll, a silver dollar, and a cigarette. She sniffed the cigarette: straight tobacco, stale. It must have been put there by Henry's son, Sam, who was eight. There was much Sherry didn't know about Henry but one thing she was sure of: he didn't smoke. Nor would he approve if he knew she did. Not that she did that often. Just when she was alone. Cigarettes helped when she was alone. Vodka helped too, as did Valium, romance novels, chocolate cherry ice cream, crying jags, shopping sprees, and her ancient, trusty, battery-operated vibrator.

Dog, Henry's dove, cooed from the rafters and flapped his dirty white wings and Sherry glanced up and shivered. What if Dog tried to land on her shoulder? He did that sometimes when Henry was home, and she always pretended it didn't scare her, pretended even to like the sharp strong beak an inch from her eyes, the claws tangled in the ends of her hair. "Nature Girl," Henry called her fondly, as she stood there, stricken. "It's just amazing to me the way Dog's taken to you. He doesn't usually like my friends."

What "friends"? Sherry thought. If only Dog were a useful bird, like a mynah or a parrot, maybe he could tell her the things she needed to know. Who was her rival? What was she like? Was she better than Sherry? Of course she was! She would not be divorced, as Sherry was, and going to law school, as Sherry was; she would not be in debt, distracted, dieting, or despondent, as Sherry so often was. This new girl would be one of those calm, clear-eyed goddesses who baked bread and looked sexy even in Birkenstocks. She would truly enjoy the things Henry enjoyed—the white-water rafting that scared Sherry speechless, the cross-country skiing that left her limping for days, the long motorcycle rides that she endured with her eyes closed.

She stared hard at the bird. "Don't come near or I'll kill you," she warned. Her voice wavered but Dog seemed to obey her; he flexed his snaky neck and flew to a rafter on the opposite side of the room. Sherry waited until she saw him settle, then quickly reviewed the contents of the mantel: the framed photo of Sam, fishing; the photo of Henry, fishing; the set of deer antlers; the Indian basket filled with matchbooks. Most of the matchbooks came from Thai restaurants and sushi bars Sherry had been to herself, with Henry, but some—Club ChiChi? what was Club ChiChi? a strip joint?—made her heart stop. She didn't want Henry at a strip joint. She didn't want Henry anywhere but right here, with her, where he belonged. When he was with her she felt solid and sturdy and unafraid; it was only when he was gone that she panicked. Henry was so handsome, so good, so sweet, and so trusting— any woman would want him. Half the time he didn't even notice how women lit up when they saw him. But Sherry did, Sherry saw it happen all the time. "Why would I want someone else," Henry had soothed her, "when I can scarcely handle you?" He'd laughed his big laugh then and added, "The fact is, most women sort of scare me. They're too needy. Too dependent. Not you. You're, I don't know, well-balanced."

The phone rang and Sherry jumped, almost screamed, then reached for it, pressing it first to her heart as she took a deep breath. "MacKay residence," she said, forcing a loud and languorous yawn. The voice on the other end was young, too young to scare anyone. "This is Jasmine?" it said. "From Sporting Life? Would you tell Henry that the collapsible fly rod he ordered just came in?" Sherry nodded, mute with relief, and then thought: *Just* came in? On a Sunday morning at 10:15? The girl hung up before she could question her, and Sherry, frowning, reached for the memo pad. There was already one name on the pad. Rochelle. Who the hell was Rochelle? A dancer at Club ChiChi? Sherry scrawled "collapsible fly rod," drew a quick, unsuccessful sketch of a fishing pole protruding from a man's fly, wadded the sketch up, and threw it into the wastepaper basket. Then she knelt by the basket and went through it. Used tissues, bottle caps, an empty box of cold tablets. No lipsticks, no tampons, no sign of Rochelle or what's-her-name. Jasmine.

She rocked back on bare heels, reached up, switched the answering machine to playback, and stared across the room at the rolltop desk. Two drawers, two cubbyholes, and, somewhere in the mess of mail on top, that lavender letter she'd seen last night while she was pouring a brandy for Henry's sore throat. It had been a hard letter to miss: big, splashy, richly perfumed, addressed in loopy purple ink with a drawing of a rose where the return address should be.

She started to walk toward the desk on her knees, but froze as the answering machine began. First there was Henry's voice, deep and slow. Just listening to him calmed her. "Gone fishin'," his voice said. "But I'll catch you later." Sherry nodded, wiped her sweaty palms on her thighs, reached for the stack of mail, then paused. It's wrong to read someone's mail, she told herself; I'll wait and hear his messages first. Henry's voice beeped off and a woman's voice came on. Sherry grimaced, lifting her face to listen as the light lisping prattle filled the room. Her grimace deepened as she recognized the words. It was her. Her own awful voice. "I hope your big bad cold is all better, hon," she was saying—imagine a grown woman talking like that!—"but if it's not it will be soon, 'cause I'm making you a pot of my grandma's special magic chicken soup, guaranteed to cure what ails you."

What crap, Sherry thought. Her grandmother had never made a pot of soup in her life. But that deli downtown did a pretty decent job; all you had to add was a handful of parsley and a few tiny bones to make the stuff look authentic. Henry had eaten three bowls and his cold had cleared up. Sort of. Not enough to permit him to kiss her good-bye when he left this morning. She narrowed her eyes, trying to remember the last time Henry had actually kissed her, one of those long soul kisses that used to make her gulp and shiver with thanks. It must have been about the same time she had had an actual unfaked orgasm. How many had she faked the last time they'd made love? Four? Five? She couldn't remember. She bowed her head and waited for the tape to end, relieved when her baby voice finally babbled its bye-byes. There were, suspiciously, no more messages on the tape; Henry must have erased them.

She craned her neck and looked up at the desk. I'll do the drawers first, she decided. She tugged at the bottom drawer—it was crammed with receipts, credit card carbons, tax records, and bank statements, all shoved in together. The thought of looking through all these frail, dimly printed papers for evidence of infidelity dismayed her. She reached for the top drawer—it was full of rocks. Big grey dirty rocks.

She rubbed her neck and stood up. Coffee, she thought. Coffee first, to give me strength for that lavender letter.

She turned the lights on in Henry's small kitchen, filled his coffee maker, and plugged it in. While she was waiting she leafed through the entries on his Endangered Species calendar on the wall: nothing there but clinic appointments for his cold at the local health center. She checked the drainboard: one cup, one plate, one fork, and poked through the plastic bucket Henry kept under the sink for compost: carrot scrapings, eggshells, apple cores. Suddenly she froze. Am I crazy? she thought.

She stood up and pushed her hair back with her elbow. Henry had given her no reason to doubt him. He was attentive and affectionate when he was with her, and if he wasn't with her all the time—well, what of it? "You ruin everything," her ex-husband had said, "with your sick suspicions." "You can't hold on to people," her best friend had said, "against their will." "You need to trust more," lover after lover had told her—but lover after lover had left, and her ex-husband had just married her best friend, and if she "sabotaged relationships"—one of her roommates had said that once—well, weren't they ripe for sabotage? "You've had some bad breaks," her last therapist had agreed, just before he killed himself, "but that's no reason to think everyone is going to abandon you. Learn to open up."

I will, Sherry thought. She pushed the garbage back under the sink and wiped her hands on her jeans. I'll just open up that lavender letter and then I'll open up myself.

She poured a cup of coffee and carried it back toward the rolltop desk. "Scat," she said shakily to Dog, who was perched on the top. "Scat, scat," she repeated, flapping one hand. Dog rose to the rafters, preened, and chuckled eerily as Sherry stared down at the mail. There was a huge stack of letters. Sierra Club. Greenpeace. Wilderness Society. Jacques Cousteau. Elizabeth Spumoni. Elizabeth who? Sherry plucked that one out and set it aside. Save the Mountain Lion. Save the Condor. Save the Spotted Owl. Nona White. Nona what? Sherry pulled Nona and set her next to Elizabeth. Friends of the Redwoods. Friends of the River. Friends of the Rainforest. Fredrica F. Hamsun.

She pushed her coffee cup back, pressed her palms together, bent her head, and opened Elizabeth's letter first. Not bad. A request for funds for the new natural history museum. Nona next. A thank-you for the canoe paddle Henry had loaned her and her husband for their trip to Oregon. Fredrica last: an invitation to a party two weeks ago, with a map, and a "Hope you can come," which Henry must have ignored, because she'd been with him that weekend; they'd gone camping with Sam.

Sherry took a deep breath and looked up from the letters. Henry hung prisms in his windows and they caught the morning sun, throwing pretty bursts of rainbows here and there over the dark disordered rooms. She exhaled, relieved. There's no one else, she thought. He's just had a cold. He's needed to be alone. He hasn't felt like making love. That's normal. That happens. It doesn't mean he's going to leave me. She stacked the letters and pushed them back. Then she realized that something was missing. Something important: the lavender letter. Her heart began to race and she could hear her own breathing, light and quick. Where was that letter?

Could Henry have taken it with him this morning? On the way out the door could he have skimmed it off the top of the desk? Why? Did he think she might read it? What sort of person did he think she was?

She put her face in her hands. A rank tangy odor rose from her palms, an odor of house dust and garbage. Looking for dirt makes you dirty— who'd told her that? Her ex-husband? One of her ex-lovers? She pressed her hands even closer to her lids, pressed so hard that a dark boggy murk seeped into her skull. Sometimes she thought that if she were ever to do what they all told her to do—if she were ever to "let go" and "open up"— that she would reveal in herself a landscape so barren, so bleak, that no one, nothing, in the world could love her. A cold marsh with salt pools and weeds and wolves roaming through it—that was her, the real her. Maybe it was the real everyone. How would she know? All she knew was that she lived there, afraid, most of the time, and no one lived with her.

She shook her head, to clear it, and brushed her fingers against the front of Henry's plaid shirt, to clean them. She felt a lump in one pocket. Curious, she plunged her hand in and fished out four packets. They were plastic coated—for honey, or mustard, or catsup—Henry was always picking up free things from restaurants, only these were flesh colored and had the word Prime written on the outside. Medicine? For his cold? Some sort of salve? A lubricant? Oh, Sherry thought. She sat very still. Condoms, she thought. She'd seen plenty of condoms; she had some herself, in her purse at this moment. It was just that she'd never expected to use them with Henry. She and Henry had an understanding. She understood that he'd always been "careful" and he understood that she had been celibate since her divorce— a lie, but that was what he believed; that was what she had told him.

So the condoms were for someone else.

She waited for the rush of satisfaction to break over her—I was right! I was right!—but all she felt was a slight gassy headache and a numb tangled pain behind her right eye. Stoic, she reached in the other pocket and pulled out a small spiral notebook. She stared at the cover. There, in Henry's big block print, were the words: Survival in the Wilderness. She opened the book. What To Do When Lost was printed on the first page. Under it Henry had written Stay Calm and nothing else. She turned to the next page. All About Frostbite was printed there with the words Don't Rub beneath it. She quickly leafed through the rest of the book. There were instructions on how to build an ice cave and snare a rabbit. Was this what Henry thought about when Henry was alone? Hypothermia and edible ferns?

She heard the motorcycle outside, jumped up, shoved the notebook back in the pocket, unbuttoned the top buttons of the shirt to get some cleavage, ran her hands through her hair to fluff it out. Bacon! she thought. She dashed into the kitchen, pulled some bacon out of the refrigerator, threw it into a pan, and turned the heat high to get the smell going fast. She took her eyeglasses off, stuck them in an empty knife drawer, and checked her face in the toaster's reflection for mascara smudge. There was a pot of basil on the windowsill; she tore off a leaf and chewed it quickly to sweeten her breath. Then the front door opened and Sam banged in. He grinned through the kitchen door, a tall, husky, red-lipped boy, already as good looking as his father.

"We must have driven a hundred miles an hour," he told her. "I think Dad was nervous about leaving you here alone."

"Really?" Sherry handed him a glass of orange juice and patted the top of his head. "I just woke up."

Sam dropped his eyes to her bare feet, which were flecked, she saw, with bits of garbage, and she crossed one over the other while she briskly mixed pancake batter. She heard Henry sneeze as he came through the front room and he sneezed again as he came into the kitchen. How handsome he was! With his hair ruffled from the wind and his cheeks flushed and that big warm smile—how handsome—and how wary! For the first time she noticed that Henry always walked on the balls of his feet, and that he held his elbows high, as if ready to turn and bolt any minute. His quick eyes moved from side to side behind his tinted goggles—surely he could take those off inside the house? She tipped her face up and dimpled.

"Kiss?" she lisped, in that pram-prattle voice. She nestled against him and after a second Henry put his arms around her; she waited until Sam was out of the room and then she laughed and said, "Oops, just a second, there's something in this shirt that's poking me; it hurts, here," and she reached in the pocket and pulled the condoms out, one by one, her expression so perplexed that Henry took off his goggles and started to laugh.

"Oh, sweetie," he said, "do you even know what these are?"

Sherry shook her head.

"They're prophylactics!" Henry said. "I got them at the clinic when I went in for my cold; they were passing them out like toothpicks, free." He dropped his voice. "I thought I'd stick a few in that secret brick for Sam; he can use them for water balloons."

"Just so long as you're not planning to use them yourself," Sherry said, her voice sweet and stern and just a trifle sad.

"Believe me," he said.

"I do," she said, surprised. She did. His arms felt good about her and his heartbeat was solid and steady. In the other room she could see Sam playing with Dog. What a picture they made, the white bird perched on the open hand of the happy child. What a nice world it was, really, or could be. It didn't have to be swamp weeds and wasteland; it could be blue skies and sunlight. She watched as Dog rose from Sam's hand to land on an old arrow quiver Henry had nailed to the wall; she smiled as the bird gave his strange whirring chuckle and pecked at something stuck in the quiver, but her smile tightened and tensed as the bird's beak tore off a long scrap of lavender paper. So that's where he'd put it.

"Something wrong, sweetie?" Henry asked, patting her.

"Not a thing, hon."

"You staggered. You don't feel faint or anything, do you?"

"No. Yes. Just a little. I must be getting your cold. I better lie down. Can you and Sam finish up in the kitchen?"

Henry nodded, led her to the couch, and covered her tenderly with a Navajo blanket. Sherry lay limp and did not open her eyes until she was sure the room was empty. Then she rose to her knees. She reached for the letter at the same moment Henry did. He stared at her. She stared back. Neither moved. And neither let go.

Can You Ever Forgive Me?

IT WAS A SHINY NEW APRIL DAY and I decided to go see Mom and Dad at the cemetery. I missed them. The drive out reminded me of them— the old summer houses at the outskirts of town were the kind of houses Mom and Dad had grown up in, houses with porches and attics and pantries and lawns, houses that we kids loved but which felt to Mom and Dad like boxy wallpapered jails. "I won't be able to breathe," Mom would promise, one hand on her heart, every time we had to visit Great Aunt Rose or Grandpa Pim in one of their large family houses. "I wish I had the nerve to break every knickknack in the place, but I don't. One of you will have to do it for me." And then turning to us as Dad parked, she would reach for me, the middle child, the most obedient, and pinching my arm, warn, *"Don't you dare,"* and Dad would chime in wearily, "Everyone behaves in this house or we'll leave you here forever."

The yards I drove past were in flower and the lawns were neatly mowed beneath the shade trees. I saw an old couple walking down the sidewalk; both wore straw hats and the man used a cane. They made me swallow with nostalgia—not for Mom and Dad, who never lived to be old—but for Aunt Rose and Grandpa Pim, whom I adored. I drove past a corner store and a grammar school with a deserted play yard. A road curving up a sudden steep hill was marked with a sign: Castle Crest Country Club. That's the road Dad would have chosen, roaring up in his Porsche, golf bag bouncing on the seat beside him; that's the road Mom would have inched up in the station wagon with her tennis skirt pleated prettily on her thighs, ready for an afternoon of vodka tonics in the bar with the girls.

But I drove straight ahead. I was the solid plodding child. The Starer. "Make her stop watching me," Mom said to Dad, and Dad put his long clean fingers over my eyes and said, "Don't scare your mother." The road dead-ended at the cemetery and I parked beneath a tree by the office. No other cars were in the lot. Two men with loosened ties were talking outside the office door; they looked as if they'd just come back from a Rotary Club luncheon and I wondered if they'd ever known Dad. They looked like the type of men Dad liked to tell jokes to, sitting behind his huge polished desk at the bank, drawling out the punch line while they waited to see if their loans were approved or not. Dad could make them laugh and as they laughed he'd tell them No, or Yes, and they often left laughing, no matter what the answer had been. That was Dad's gift, Mom said, to charm small men with small minds.

"When I think of the boys I could have married." Mom, drink in hand, would tip up her face and recite the names of her ex-fiancés, familiar as the names of our grade school teachers: Woody Melody. Max Robinson. Harlan Hymes. Woody, Mom said, was a university professor. Max was a heart specialist. And Harlan was a famous voice on commercials.

"I gave them all back their rings," Mom would say. "I broke their hearts. I had to. They were nice boys but they were no match for your father. Who knows why? It's a mystery to me."

I looked down at my own ringless hand—my brothers married long ago and moved away, but I stay on, the same—and tucked in my blouse. It was red, which was inappropriate, probably, for a graveside visit, and wrinkled; there was taco sauce from lunch on one cuff so I rolled both sleeves up. Neither Mom nor Dad would approve of the way I looked today. "Is that a statement?" Dad used to ask, peering over his glasses as I walked in their house in tank top and cutoffs. "Or an advertisement?" "Is it so hard," Mom would echo, mascara dotting the moist pale skin of her cheek, "to look like a lady?"

Yes, then. And yes, now. Already defensive, I stepped out of the car and slammed the door. The two men looked over, expectant: did I need directions? I shouldered my purse and shook my head. I knew where Mom and Dad were; I'd been here before, first when Mom died two years ago, then again last October, when the white limousine hired by Dad's girlfriend delivered his ashes in a grand show of wealth and waste and open-mindedness. I turned toward the right.

The cemetery was as complex as a city, with little neighborhoods and warrens and corner clusters of its own. The older part, the meadow where the flat headstones lay, was being mowed by Mexican workers with earphones. I watched one of them mow around a dwarfed weeping willow; the little tree startled me, so stylized, so grotesque, like something left over from Queen Victoria's childhood. Oh, I thought, suddenly, this is where the dead people are buried. The thought stopped me and made me want to giggle. Contrite and careful, I walked past the hard marble benches dedicated to the long gone, through the low, closely packed crypts, placed like filing cabinets in an outdoor office, toward the long granite wall where Mom and Dad had been housed on a shelf. I ducked under another stunted tree, a hawthorn of some sort, humped with thick clusters of odorless pink blooms, and read the inscription on the tombstone beneath it. Can You Ever Forgive Me? was carved into the stone and I stepped back, repelled. That seemed a terrible question to ask from the grave. Who had done what to whom? I hurried on. The wall I approached was hung with bouquets so bright they seemed real, seasonal sprays of lilac and rose and daffodil. Mom and Dad would never have had plastic flowers in their home but you got used to them here, they looked appropriate here, and I hoped the little bunch of lupine and forget-me-nots I had brought last October had held up through the winter. What if it was damaged? What if Mom and Dad were damaged? What if they weren't even there?

I rounded the corner of the wall, looked up, and smiled with relief. "Hi," I said. They were there. Too high to touch, a few feet over my head, boxed together in a granite drawer marked with two plaques, Mom's brass dates already fading, Dad's rudely new. I was very glad to see them. The flowers I had bought last year, except for a dingy drapery of spiderweb on one side, looked just fine; the purply blue, turquoise, azure, and white combination was probably not what Mom and Dad would have chosen, but it looked much nicer than the dried out twigs of holly stuck in Angelo Dominguez's vase to the right or the hideous stalk of magenta sweet peas arcing crazily out of Judith Norfund's vase to the left.

I crossed my arms and craned my neck, smiling like a fool as I gazed up, glad to be here with my two dear ones. You're still the classiest guys in the joint, I told them. I felt myself fill up with feeling, solidly, as if I had been empty before and was now being completed. The feeling was pleasurable for about a second, then drained away. I was not sure what to do next. I tried a few lines of the Lord's Prayer but stopped; Mom and Dad were agnostics. The Serenity Prayer would irritate them too. Where did you learn that? they'd ask. In a twelve-step what? I wondered if I should try to strike up some small talk with the wall, but we had never been a family who communicated well. Dad's idea of conversation had been to say, "Hey did you see that cartoon in the *New Yorker*?" followed by a richly inappropriate chuckle whether I had or had not, and my mother's often brilliant talk had been centered, almost to the very end, on herself. What could I tell them?

I got the afternoon off, I began. My boss is out of town so I took off. It's all right. The answering service will cover. He won't mind. Really. It's nothing I'll get fired for or anything. School is going well. I might even graduate one of these years. I'm still in journalism and you'd be proud: I had an article on the front page last week. No, not of the city paper. The college paper. One of the college papers. Anyway they gave me a byline. And it's over with Harley; you didn't know Harley but you wouldn't have liked him. He's back with his wife. Some girlfriends and I are going to go to Reno—I know, Reno—still it should be fun; I won't gamble.

I waited for a response but the wall met me blankly. I never had held their attention. I had started to lie, like I always had, and I was beginning to get a crick in my neck, and when I yawned I knew it was time to move on. The spiderweb bothered me though and I thought as long as I had come this far I ought to make myself useful, so I looked around for a pole or grappling hook so I could reach up and get the vase down and dust it off. "I'll be right back," I told them. Without warning I saw them exactly as they used to look when I'd come up to their house to cook dinner during Mom's last year—Dad affable behind the paper, smoking cigarette after cigarette, Mom perfumed and sober after an afternoon nap, sitting up on her pillows, full of little orders given gaily. "I don't know what I'd do without you," she would say as she watched me walk in with groceries, "I'd just be stuck with Mr. Grouch here," and then in one of her sudden mood swirls she would start to cry and Dad would say, "You see what I go through?" not looking up from his paper.

Maybe he was having an affair then, I thought, as I turned away to look for the grappling hook. Maybe he was already seeing the woman he moved in with six months after Mom died; he denied he had been but who would tell their own child something like that? "I never let one of them touch me," Mom bragged of her ex-fiancés—but she kissed all her friends' husbands in the kitchen at parties; I used to see her. I also saw her and Dad once, at a party, dancing in the garden with their arms around each other; after they left I went out to the garden myself and danced alone in my nightgown. I could imagine Mom now, sitting up on her pillows, grilling Dad about the two long years she'd been alone in the crypt. "Did you at least take Doll Watson to the Follies?" she'd nag, or, "I always thought you had a little sneaker for Pinkie Monroe; did she come on to you once I was out of the way? Tell me the truth."

"I won't tell you anything," Dad would answer lightly, politely, and turn a page of his paper. The girlfriend he'd ended up with would never occur to Mom. She was not the sort of person Mom could invent. She was a big tall blond, a Palm Springs real estate agent who rode stallions in horse shows, when she was sober, which was not that often; she had taken good care of Dad and he would never betray her to anyone. He would simply sit behind his paper, as packed with secrets as he'd been when he'd returned from Paris after World War II, and Mom could pose and pout until she wore out.

I walked toward a fountain that dished out small plates of water at a uniform rate as it spun; the water made no music, or none that I could hear above the din of the mowers. A pole was propped beside it; as I picked it up I saw a name I recognized on one of the neighboring crypts: Clive Caswell. Clive was one of the men Mom had kissed. I wondered if other friends were here. They should be, I thought; all of them drank and smoked as much as Mom and Dad. Maybe their ghosts got together on full moon nights by the weeping willow tree in the meadow, the men in white shoes and plaid golf pants, the women swinging their perky bruised legs on the tombstones as they eyed each other's hairdos.

I carried the grappling hook back to the crypt wall, reached up, grasped the metal flower holder on the first try, and brought it down. That seemed wrong, to do something on the first try with Mom and Dad looking. They hadn't let me dry knives until I was ten. "Clive's here," I said, to distract them. I lifted the flowers out and brushed the spiderwebs off against the damp green edge of the lawn. A black spider tumbled out and I tossed it aside, too intent to care if it was a black widow or not. It was simply a nuisance. Glancing inside the vase was a bad idea, for it was dark and deep and filled with ancient dirt, and the idea of what my parents really were doing behind their plaqued resting place, neither reading nor dimpling against lace pillows, but lying soulless in an ashy rubble of bone and tooth chips, flitted into my mind and exited like the spider, too quickly to teach me anything. I straightened, pleased with my housekeeping contribution, and replaced the flowers. They looked fine. Mom and Dad were glad I had come and done that for them. With the edge of the pole I scraped off a few extra webby growths around the plaque and then I nudged Judith Norfund's pushy sweet peas back; she was trying to hog my parents' space; people were always trying to get too close to them, take some of the glamour and courage the two of them had, at their best. They were drunks, a stubborn voice in my head insisted. Your mother used to hit you in the face with a hairbrush. Your father called you a stupid whore. They killed themselves with their addictions and angers and they did their best to kill you too.

I know that, I admitted. But still, looking up I felt a surge of the old love, the wild blood love that is as unstoppable as vomit or laughter. For these two people I would fall to my knees, tear my hair, blacken my face, abase myself, howl. "I love you," I said to Mom and Dad. The mowers had stopped and I could hear my own voice, as unformed as a child's. I waved, like I used to, when I was a little girl at the window and they were spinning entwined in the garden. I love you I love you I love you.

I turned then and left. As I passed the tomb under the pink tree one of the mowers walked past; his black hair swung in a braid and when he turned to look at me I saw with a shock he had bright warm eyes and a dimple and I smiled back before I could help it. Oh, oh, I thought. I'm in trouble now. If Mom and Dad hear I went home with the gardener...

Eyes down, I hurried, almost ran, to my car.

Untitled

IT WAS THE LAST STRETCH of the spring semester and she would not return to teach in the fall. Nobody told her. She heard from a student. Mitzi Perls strode into her office and flung the fall schedule onto the desk. "I have the worst luck," Mitzi said. "Here I finally find a writing teacher who lets me do dragons, and look what happens: they fire you."

Ellen looked at the schedule. Mitzi was right. She handed it back, surprised by the expectant expression in Mitzi's dark eyes. Is she afraid I'll burst into tears? Ellen thought.

"It's all right," she heard herself say.

"Everything happens to me," Mitzi answered.

Ellen's office was in the basement of the women's gym and she was used to the noise of running feet, rock music, and the more intimate sounds of the toilet. The low-ceilinged, windowless room contained an empty book-case, an empty file cabinet, and four metal desks. There were so few signs of life in the room—no house plants or coffee cups—that Ellen had long since stopped wondering about her office mates. She had never met them, and she had begun to treat the office as if she alone owned it. After Mitzi left, she got up and carefully straightened the posters of Virginia Woolf and Willa Cather she had taped to the wall; she had known, when she put them up, that she would have to take them down someday. That was the risk you took when you agreed to teach in a state university. Your corners got torn. You got a little bent. She sat down and reread the schedule Mitzi had left on her desk. Two other part-timers, both poets, were being retained, but both, Ellen remembered, had been hired a semester before she had. Karl Pepper, Wolf Whitsun, Rita Arakis, Dirk McDonnell—the familiar names of tenured professors crowding the page made her feel like an outsider, a student again. She turned the schedule over and picked up a pen. $500, she wrote on the back. That was the overdue child support. She had a small grant coming in June. There was the typing job at six dollars an hour and whatever Kip chipped in. She should be able to get something from unemployment. She had planned to waitress this summer anyway.

On her way to class she checked her mail slot. There was no notice of dismissal. There was nothing but two late stories from students and a note from Karl. Ellen slid the mail into her book bag and walked down the hall, but when she came to the door of Dr. Strommer's office she stopped. The door was unlocked and swung ajar at her light tap. The head of the creative writing department was alone at his desk, unwrapping a packet of chocolate chip cookies. Ellen smiled hesitantly. She had taught short story writing for five semesters now, but she was not sure Dr. Strommer knew who she was. When they passed in the halls his face took on the dreamy, intent expression of a child tonguing a loose tooth. "I'm Ellen Trennel," she said. "I hear I've been fired."

"Fired?"

"I'm not on the schedule."

She waited for him to say, Not true. Instead he fingered the packet of cookies. Ellen saw a bag of potting mix on the floor beneath his desk, a sheriff's star on the wall, a print of "The Peaceable Kingdom" over the desk. "I don't like the word *fired*," he said.

Ellen felt reckless. "Canned," she said. "Axed."

Dr. Strommer, expressionless, stared past her. "I like the word *not rehired*," he said. "If the budget changes, which is, granted, unlikely, we may still be able to factor you in."

Ellen, stubborn, said, "I heard from a student."

"Students are not supposed to have access to the data yet."

It was not an apology but Ellen saw it would have to do. She was late for her class. As she turned to go she consoled herself with the thought that at least he'd know who she was the next time they passed in the halls. Or would he? His expression was benign but blank and she would not be in the halls much longer. She heard him reach for the cookies as she walked out the door.

Her classroom was large, long, and low-ceilinged, with three walls of chalkboard and one full wall of windows hung with tiers of collapsed metal blinds. The students sat at four tables that had been joined corner to corner to form a square. The empty space in the center of the square made Ellen uneasy, for she could think of no way to use it. We could throw all the stories in and have a bonfire, she thought. She had thirty-one students and twenty-nine chairs. Mitzi Perls crouched on the floor whether she was early or late, her dark eyes flashing through her tangled bangs. Ellen herself always stood. It was easier to see the students' faces, and she liked to move around as she talked and read. She was no longer physically afraid of her students—that had passed after the first semester—and she was almost used to the sound of her own voice in a silent room, although it still shocked her at times, it was so unconvincing and girlish. When students took notes she always wondered what they were writing down, really, and she had to fight the temptation to read over their shoulders.

The class was structured simply. Student stories were read out loud and then discussed. The very good and the very poor stories were greeted with the same dropped eyes and long silences, but the mediocre stories raised questions of craft the class liked to discuss. Ellen had to watch that Enid, knitting as she listened, did not limit the critique of Sarah's story about a nun who had AIDS to a discussion of medical terms; she had to see that Victor, slouched by the windows, stayed awake, and that Peter Gage, who worked nights, did not wake up. She had to make sure that Harry Hoagman, a reentry student in his sixties, did not compare Jack Hughes's mountain climbing story to his own experiences in Colorado in 1955; she had to hope that Serafina did not giggle too rapturously, too often. She had to give Mitzi her chance to say why she could no longer relate to human characters, and she had to clear a space of silence at the end of every session so that Sandy Danziger could swiftly, softly, make the same comments that Ellen herself had worked out in painstaking detail on every manuscript she gave back.

The note from Karl said, "I never see you. You must be working too hard. How about coffee?" Since Karl himself drank only herbal teas, his insistence on calling their weekly meetings "coffee dates" was confusing to

Ellen. If Karl proposed coffee but ordered tea, what was he asking for really? Did he know? Did she want to know? No, and no. Quickly, to cover her alarm at the way Karl leapt up to pull a chair out for her in the café, she told him about her meeting with Dr. Strommer.

"Ron's a fool," Karl said. "Doesn't he know what a treasure you are?"

Ellen flushed, gratified. "Guess not," she said.

"There are ways we could fight this," Karl said. "If you want. Do you want?"

"I don't know," Ellen answered. Karl, she knew, was a fighter. He had a fighter's thick, quick body and broken nose; he'd been active in the university riots two decades before and had been photographed, famously, for reading Thoreau to a cop in a gas mask.

"Let me put it another way," Karl said. "Do you want to teach?"

Ellen thought. "I need the job."

"Then get your class to write letters. Have them sign a petition. Students love to sign petitions. Have them march on Ron's office. Do a little politicking."

Ellen nodded, her eyes downcast. Karl's last novel had been about Watergate, and she'd had to skip whole chapters of "politics," she'd been so confused and bored. Karl blew on his tea, retied the shoelace on his jogging shoes, and began to talk about hiring a lawyer, suing the regents, organizing other lecturers, having a rally. "You'd lose of course," he summed up, "but you'd sure shake the system." He saw Ellen's face and clucked her lightly under the chin. "Cheer up darling," he said, "if you don't want to change the world, you don't have to."

He walked her back across campus to her car. At the curb—a habit they had slipped into months before—he leaned forward and kissed her goodbye. His kisses were firm and warm and so pleasant that Ellen sometimes thought she would just say the hell with it and fall in love with him. It would be very easy. But Karl had a wife. And she had two children. And Kip; she had Kip. For a little while longer.

Sometimes she would wake up at night and Kip would be gone and then she would practice, toeing through the empty sheets. Testing, testing, she would think, her foot finding the hollow he'd left on his side. She knew if she turned she'd see him standing by the window, thin and high-shouldered, outlined in moonlight. He would be thinking about leaving her. He had been thinking about leaving her for months now, not because he didn't love her, he said, nor because he didn't love her children, he said, but because living in an old house in a rundown neighborhood with a ready-made family was not living, exactly. Living, real living, involved making money. Kip had been thinking about money—"big money," he called it—ever since his thirtieth birthday, and the thinking had aged him. Ellen no longer recognized this pale, hollow-eyed man as the playful boy she had met at a writers' conference the summer before; she had to look through their snapshots to see Kip romping with the dog, mugging with her kids, smiling into the sun straight up at her. Now when he smiled he looked like a skull. One of his friends at the film institute had just sold a script to George Lucas; another friend had an option from Disney. When yet another friend sold a sitcom pilot to a television network, Kip drove out to the beach and slept in his car for two nights; when he returned he cut his long hair, removed his one earring, and joined a health club where he played racquetball viciously for hours.

Sometimes he took her to parties where he and other instructors from the film institute gathered to drink and get high and go through their rushes again and again. Ellen sat tensely in the flickering dark, worried about the baby-sitter, wishing she were home, at her own desk, before her own typewriter. "If that's what you wish," Kip would say, exasperated, "why aren't you there? If you know what you want to do, why don't you do it?"

And Ellen always shrugged, as she shrugged now, waving good-bye to Karl at the corner. She didn't know why she wasn't doing what she wanted to do. Things that seemed simple for others were not simple for her. Maybe if she'd gone to Greece at nineteen, as she'd meant to. Maybe if she'd never fallen in love with her ex-husband, never had children, never started teaching, never met Kip—maybe then she would be doing what she wanted to do.

More and more she was thinking all she wanted to do was sit with her hands clasped and stare into space forever.

In the meantime, there was dinner. Ellen drove to the store, Karl's kiss still damp on her lips, picked up some groceries, drove to the child care center, picked up her children, dropped her son at the soccer field, her daughter at the orthodontist, drove back to the field to cheer the game, back to the orthodontist to explain why her payment had to be late on the new braces. It was dark by the time she got home. She had the two children help her carry groceries in, called to Kip, who was doing something in the bedroom, calmed the dog, who had been locked in the bathroom, started to cook. At dinner they all talked about their day. "I lost my job," she said, when her turn came.

"Which one?" the children asked.

"The teaching job."

"Did you do something wrong?"

"No. Of course not."

Her son nodded, convinced, but her daughter stared. "They could not factor me in," Ellen said. She waited but neither child questioned the expression; perhaps it was one they knew. Relieved, she asked who wanted salad. I'm a terrible teacher, she thought. I hate to explain things. She set the salad bowl down and found Kip's eyes on her; he'd been quiet all evening.

"We're both free then," he said. "I gave my notice at the institute this morning. Why don't you come with me to Tokyo?"

"Tokyo?" Ellen stared. She had thought when Kip left her he would go to New York or Paris. She had not thought of Tokyo. "When?" she said.

"Tonight."

Ellen, startled, laughed. The children laughed too. Kip dropped his eyes and pushed back his plate.

"You just quit the institute in midsemester?" Ellen said. "Don't you have a commitment there?"

"Commitments can be broken," Kip said. "As you've learned."

"I guess," Ellen said. She waited. "What are you going to do in Tokyo?" she asked after a minute.

"I'm going to make language films for businessmen."

Ellen couldn't help it; she laughed again.

She missed him more than she thought she would. She lost weight, couldn't concentrate, was sharp with the children, backed into the garage door, wrote August instead of April on her checkbook—little things, but they alarmed her. Was this the way she was going to age? She came to class with coffee stains on her skirt, one earring lost; she was always checking her purse to make sure of her keys. She had never felt so eccentric. I am getting like Josephine Johnson, she thought. But Josephine Johnson had earned her old-ladyhood; she was seventy years old. She carried a string bag, wore two prominent hearing aids and a huge man's watch, pulled a red Tam o' Shanter over her thick grey bob. Ellen sat at her desk in the basement below the gym, glad to listen to Josephine instead of her own tired thoughts.

"I never had a doggone minute to call my own," Josephine told her, "until I was fifty years old. Then in two short blessed days my Daddy died and my brother Will went to jail and there I was, all alone in the house at last. Didn't know what I wanted to do, did know I wanted to write. So I started college. That was twenty years ago," Josephine said, "and I'm hoping to write for twenty more." She handed Ellen a one-page story. It was titled "How the Skunk Got His Stink" and was written in dialect. Ellen scanned it, smiling, until she came to the last line: "So dats why de skunk sometimes stinks like de nigger."

"Oh, no," Ellen said. She put the story down and looked at Josephine who beamed proudly back. "This is unacceptable," Ellen said.

Josephine nodded and turned her hearing aids up. "Joel Chandler Harris," she said. "He helped my style."

"It's not your style," Ellen said. "It's your..." She stared into Josephine's round blue eyes. Your what? Your whole harsh, hard, ignorant life?

"See this word?" she said. Josephine followed her finger, said, "Oh, of course," reached for the paper, and wrote *Afro-American* instead.

"No," Ellen groaned, "no, no, never, no." She began talking and talked for almost an hour but when Josephine left she still wasn't sure if anything had sunk in. I need something, Ellen thought, to help my own "style." A bullet of aspirin. A triple martini. Some of Serafina's marijuana.

Serafina seemed to smoke her dope at the break because her laughter, always bubbling in the background, boiled over toward the end of every period. Serafina wore bangles on her arms and seashells in her hair and when she laughed she tinkled all over; the effect was pretty but so disruptive Ellen found herself adopting a stern, stiff attitude toward the girl in an effort to sober her up. The attempt did not work. After class Serafina often came up and kissed Ellen on the cheek; Ellen could get a contact high from Serafina's breath alone. "You're so sweet," Serafina breathed. "You're just too sweet to teach."

"That seems to be what everyone thinks," Ellen said. "Did you finish your story?"

"I did, yes, I finished the one about the vampire, but I can't finish the one about the squid. Do you think there could be such a thing as a vampire squid?"

"Of course," said Ellen. She had just spent three hours discussing questions like: Can a girl with "amethyst eyes" have a "piercing obsidian gaze"? "A vampire squid is a distinct possibility."

"Good," said Serafina. "Now all I need is a title."

Ellen nodded. For some reason, all her students' stories were titled "Untitled" this semester. That name was in vogue. The wildest story—the one about the Siamese twins joined at the heart who tried to kill an Elvis impersonator in a tanning booth—and the mildest, about the old woman setting the table for her ten cats—were both titled "Untitled." It was a problem with focus, Ellen told the class. Or conviction. Or clarity. Or something. How should I know, Ellen thought. Creative writing—she had said this a hundred times—could not be taught. Or maybe it could. Just not by her.

"I enjoyed your comments on my story and then I looked up and saw this mark at the top? This B—? I don't know how to take that, at first I thought it was just a doodle you'd made? Was it a doodle?"

"No," said Ellen. "It was your grade."

"I don't accept grades," explained Enid Warwick. She sat down by Ellen's desk and drew her knitting out of a big black purse. "I mean, how can you grade a creative work to begin with? It's not like I wrote a book report. Or a term paper. I just would like to know what your standards are. I know you explained at the beginning of the class that you had certain standards but unless you give everyone else an F, I don't see how you can justify giving me a B—. I mean there are a lot of, let's face it, beginning writers in your class. I am not a beginning writer. I came to see you privately today because I don't like to put you on the spot in front of everyone, but you ought to know that I've been writing ever since I was eight years old and I've had several poems published. When I was twelve my teacher sent a poem I'd written to a magazine and it won a contest. My parents were very strict and when they found out I'd won a contest they locked me in my room for six weeks. They took all my books and paper away. I wrote on toilet paper. So you see how seriously I am committed. I had to laugh when I saw your note saying this story was 'unconvincing.' Because I hate to tell you, Professor Trennel, but everything in this story is true. It's not made up. Here, where the woman goes into the hospital for the 'unspecified blood disease' and you've written 'flat' in the margin? Well that really happened. To me. I have a rare blood disease. I have my own hematologist and I have to see him for tests three times a year. Also here where I wrote, 'she just wanted to lay down,' and you crossed out 'lay' and wrote 'lie'? I did that on purpose. I wanted to show her exhaustion. Also here where I've used the small letter *i* for I and you've capitalized it? Well that has a purpose too, that's to show my heroine's low self-esteem. She thinks so little of herself she can't give herself a big I. Don't you get it? I felt certain you'd get it."

"No," said Ellen. And then, despite herself, "Sorry."

"I don't accept 'sorry,'" said Enid Warwick, knitting.

Would you accept a punch in the mouth? Would you accept your manuscript wadded up and returned with the footprint it deserves on each page? Would you accept...Easy, thought Ellen. Relax. Be patient with the patients. It was wrong, she knew, to think of some of her students as patients and yet...Andy Jones came in as Enid left. Andy Jones was six feet four with hunched shoulders, strangler's hands, and a loose slipping smile. He'd been writing, he told her, just not on paper. "I do my best work," he said, "in my head." Ellen remembered his first story: five pornographic paragraphs written in longhand on the back of a lunch sack. There had been no second story. Now, a week before the third story was due, he stood pressed to her desk, his smile twitching like a jump rope across his face. "I got a crazy idea," he said. "All I need to do is type it up." He leaned close. "You believe me, don't you?" he asked. Ellen listened to the bounce of a basketball on the courts above them.

"I believe you," she said, her voice steady. Andy turned and walked out. She never saw him again.

Leah was a patient of another sort; she wasn't insane and she wasn't scary; she was sick and probably dying of muscular sclerosis. The disease had been diagnosed a year ago and Leah told Ellen she was "almost disappointed" that more had not happened since. "I'm supposed to go blind, you know," Leah said, "It could happen any time." She sighed and smoothed her skirt over her round brown legs. She was nineteen years old. "I can't write fiction anymore," she said. "Every time I try to write I fall asleep. I've been having unbelievable dreams."

"You could write your dreams down," Ellen suggested.

"I could do that. But I don't think I'm going to. I would like to come in and see you during office hours though. Just to talk. Would that be all right?"

"Of course," Ellen said. But it wasn't. Too many others needed her time. Victor slouched and smoked outside in the hall and Alvin slid by the door and Sandy Danziger paced back and forth while Leah fingered her healing crystal, eyes closed, and talked on. "My parents are sending me to Florence this summer," Leah told Ellen. "Florence is the carrot. They are saying, Be a good little donkey and don't kill yourself, and look what we'll give you."

The first time Ellen heard this she was moved. The second time, Ellen thought, That's all right, she needs to get it out. The third time, Ellen thought, I wonder if I left my sunglasses in the car.

If some of the students were patients, at least two were writers. Victor was a writer. Victor, slouched in the back with his old leather jacket and his new black eye and his packet of Camels was the most talented student she had ever had. He was twenty-two, he told her, "going on sixteen." He was handsome, affected, stagy, cupping his small white hands around his cigarette even when lighting it in the lucid airless hall outside the classroom. He told Ellen that he supported himself as a prostitute and Ellen winced with disbelief. No one, she thought, would do that in this day and age—would they? Victor smiled sleepily and said he sometimes made five hundred dollars a night. Then he asked her for a quarter to catch the bus home. Ellen watched him swagger off, her face tight with worry. He had just handed her a sad, spare story about a boy who deliberately seduces his best friend. Not a word was out of place.

The other writer among her students was Sandy Danziger. Sandy was a doctor's wife; she wore suede slacks and silk blouses and her lips were parched from the antidepressants she sucked like breath mints. She spoke so quietly that Ellen sometimes felt she was eavesdropping on night thoughts she had no business hearing. "I want to be good," Sandy said. "Do you think I can be good? Really good?"

"Yes," Ellen said.

"As good as you?"

"Why would you want to...?" Ellen paused. "You can be as good as you want to be," she said.

"How? What do I do? Tell me what to do." Sandy sat perfectly still in a hot cloud of Shalimar while Ellen told her she had to focus her life so it centered on writing. "You'll need child care," Ellen heard herself say. "And someone to help with the house. You'll need a room or an office of your own and you'll need time alone—hours each day—to concentrate. You'll need," she said, "to take yourself seriously."

Sandy twisted her rings and nodded. Ellen stared at the manuscript on the desk between them. It was a glamorous, perverse, obsessive narrative. Ellen had not been able to put it down, she could not wait to read more. When Sandy, in that sleepwalker's voice, said, or seemed to say, "So what am I writing, exactly?" her own voice was impatient.

"You are writing chapter one," she said.

After Sandy, Ellen rubbed her eyes and slumped down on her desk. Sandy worked fast. She was one of those writers who bloomed at one touch. She would be halfway home in her BMW by now. She would have a brand new laptop in the trunk of the car, and the keys to a quiet office with an ocean view on the seat beside her. By nine tonight she would have finished chapter two and by this time next week the whole book would be finished and sold to the movies while she, Ellen, was still writing careful answers to the last question on grant proposals: "Describe how having these funds would affect your career."

"If you want to be a better writer," Ellen said, "listen up. I'll give you some guidelines." She had everyone's full attention. Well, not everyone's. Peter Gage still slept and Serafina was slipping belled bracelets on and off Josephine Johnson's freckled, outstretched arm. Ellen crossed her arms and paced through her list. It was a short list.

Don't start a story with your character waking up in bed in the morning. Don't have anyone look into a bathroom mirror. Don't say "four-door four-cylinder Chevy Citation" when you can say "car." All right is two words no matter what the dictionary says. Remember that strong words—like *fuck*— lose their effectiveness when repeated. Commas go inside quotes when followed by attributives. If you are ever tempted to put your head to the keyboard and laugh out loud at what you've just written, you probably shouldn't drink wine while you're working. Don't ever say: "Something deep inside her said." Avoid the word *got*, avoid the word *gut*, avoid the word *snuck*. *Drugged* is not the past tense of *drag*, though it should be. Don't change tense in midstory or point of view in midparagraph. Plagiarize only from pros. Show don't tell. If you don't know what to write about, write about something you don't know about. Never, ever, end a story with, "And then I woke up."

"I like stories that scare me," Serafina said. "Like Stephen King stories?" She shivered daintily; her seashells chimed. Her eyes were red, her pupils were huge, she smelled like a campfire put out in a cave.

"I like stories that entertain," Harry Hoagman said. "Good solid stories about baseball. Or war."

"I like stories about children," said Enid Warwick.

"I like stories about children too," said Victor.

"Not that kind of story," said Sandy Danziger.

"Sometimes I think I'd like to write, you know, about a girl who falls in love with a guy and the guy falls in love with her, and they get married and live happily forever after," said Leah.

"I don't remember any stories I've liked," said Alvin. "I mainly watch TV." He ducked his head and gulped. There was something wrong with Alvin; he was too plump, too limp, his cheeks were too damp, his glasses too thick. He came up to Ellen at the end of every class, his eyes on the floor, his fingertips pleating the air as he spoke. "Now let me see if I understand this," he'd say. "The assignment is due today, right? And you want it double-spaced? On white paper?" The problem was, Ellen knew, that Alvin was frightened and did not belong in this class. He was younger than the other students; he had not taken the prerequisite English courses, his vocabulary and imagery were limited to the cartoons he had watched all his life.

"So why did you let him enroll?" Karl asked when Ellen made the mistake of mentioning that Alvin annoyed her. "You had every right to refuse him admittance." Ellen tried to explain how Alvin had returned week after week with his soiled Admit Slip, and how she had finally given in, but Karl shook his head and Ellen knew what he was thinking. He was thinking that Alvin, soft pale sticky little Alvin, was smarter than she was. And he was right.

"You know if you want to keep this job," Karl said, "it wouldn't hurt to show up at a department meeting once in a while."

So she went. Took the one afternoon she had free to write on her novel and went to a faculty meeting. She was one of the first in the committee room. Dr. Strommer gave her his remote smile; a famous woman poet said, "I love your skirt." Two other part-timers glanced at her darkly. Both seemed dressed in some sort of costume: black turtlenecks, tweed jackets; both carried briefcases. Karl came in and sat down beside her. "Why do you always sit in the back?" he complained. He looked brown and fit; his blue work shirt smelled like sunshine, even his jogging shoes looked laundered. None of the other tenured professors looked as healthy as he did; most of them looked elderly and ill and as unhappy as cats to be crammed in together. If I knew them better, Ellen reminded herself, I would like them more; it's just that after five semesters I don't know them at all. She skimmed their sour faces. When was the last time one of these men had published a novel? Or won an award? Or looked upon their chosen profession with anything like joy? Perhaps they had started out, as she had started out, on a whim. You hear about a position, you apply, you have an interview, it's yours, a joke job, bad hours, rotten pay; the joke wears thin but you come back anyway, year after year. She frowned. Everyone in this room is second rate, she thought, adding, loyally, except Karl. I am second rate myself. That's the real joke, she thought. I fit right in. I've found my niche, and my niche knows me not.

After the meeting, Karl walked her back to her car. She drove an old station wagon, a legacy from her marriage, with a basket of dirty clothes to take to the Laundromat on the passenger seat. She didn't want Karl to see the clothes, or the mail on the dashboard that contained two rejection notices, a note from her ex-husband saying he would not be able to take the children for the summer after all, a snapshot of Kip in front of a pagoda, a letter from her agent saying the paperback rights on her novel had not been sold, and a returned check from the supermarket. Karl gave her one of his wonderful kisses as they stood on the sidewalk. It was sugary, soft in the center, and opened like the eye of a frosted Easter egg into Karl's world, which Ellen saw for the first time had a small safe place for her. All she had to do was say yes and step in. She sighed and pulled back. She drove home deeply depressed and so hungry with lust she could have gnawed on the sunset.

What did she want? Her children, of course. They slept with her sometimes, after Kip left, one on each side, with the dog at the foot. She woke up with bubble gum in her hair, whispers in her ears, wet toothy kisses. Worth it, all worth it. What else did she need? Her books? Yes. Her beloved old IBM Selectric that she could not afford to replace with a word processor? Yes. Her privacy? Yes. Time to write? Yes and yes and yes. Kip? She didn't know. Someone else? She didn't know. It felt nice, alone; it felt good, it felt easy; she liked it like this. What did that make her? Selfish? Unfeeling? But weren't selfish unfeeling people supposed to be successful? Why wasn't she successful? She'd had a novel published, it had sold five thousand copies, it had had good reviews. Weren't published novelists with good reviews successful? Weren't they valued as teachers? Why wasn't she valued?

"Go to Strommer," Karl said. Tell him you've thrown together a course on, oh, say, contemporary California women authors. See if he'll hire you to teach it."

"Oh, Karl," Ellen said, "I hate contemporary California women authors."

"I give up," Karl said.

Ellen nodded. She knew that he meant it.

The last day of school she brought two jugs of wine and a loaf of home-baked bread to the classroom. Sandy brought chocolate truffles individually wrapped in gold paper. Enid Warwick brought a bag of prunes. Serafina tinkled around the desks and pressed a Hershey's Kiss into everyone's palm, two into Ellen's. There were still a few stories to read and discuss. Harry Hoagman read a story about a trip he and his wife had taken to visit their married daughter on Amtrak; it was called "A Trainful Experience" and was the first story he, or anyone else, had titled in weeks. Victor threw down a third glass of wine and read a story about a thirteen-year-old girl who was raped so brutally she aborted. Josephine Johnson read a story about a talking tide pool and Mitzi read a story about a vegetarian dragon and Peter Gage, who had not said a single word all semester, read a perfect story about his dying father, and that was it, the last class was over. Ellen exchanged good-byes with the students who came up to thank her; she kissed Serafina, pushed the address of her own agent into Sandy's jeweled hand, gave Victor a dollar for cigarettes, said "Good luck" even to Enid Warwick. She urged students who were staying in the city to meet together in writing groups over the summer. Her own summer plans, she said, included working on her novel and hostessing at Jerry's Chop House. "It's a crime you won't be teaching next fall," three or four of her worst students said, and Ellen, airy, said, "You never can tell. I may be back."

She wondered if she would. It didn't seem likely. She waited until the classroom emptied and then she dropped the wine bottles into the wastepaper basket and walked back down the hall. On the way out, she stopped at her mail slot. She was surprised, and, for a second, delighted, to see a memo from Dr. Strommer. Maybe he wanted to thank her. Maybe he was asking her to stay. But even before she opened it, she knew what the memo would say. It would say, simply, that the department was not prepared to offer a course in contemporary California women authors at this point in time. She read it through, crushed it, threw it away.

It was sunny outside and the campus looked huge and handsome and unfamiliar, with students in cutoffs and sunglasses playing Frisbee on the lawn and rock music pouring from speakers set around the quad. Bright flowers bloomed along the paths and the air smelled like cut grass. Ellen walked slowly, feeling sadder than she meant to feel. What after all could she want from this place? A happy ending? A fairy-tale finish? She remembered the last lines of Serafina's squid story: "The scary demon, oozing icky blood, collapsed in the corner and Captain Hansome turned to me and said,

'Why don't you pack a bag, honey, and I'll make reservations to get us a motel in Las Vegas. We can enjoy exotic foods there and alcoholic beverages.' The End."

The end, Ellen repeated. Two good words, and true. She looked down to see Alvin standing before her, dewy with fear. "What are we doing?" he asked. "Are we meeting outside? Are we having a final?"

"No," Ellen said. She touched his arm, to calm him. "We're going home now," she said. "We're through."

About the Author

MOLLY GILES, with her keen eye and ear for a story, is soon to be an acclaimed writer of our times. Nominated for a Pulitzer Prize, Giles's first collection, *Rough Translations*, received the Flannery O'Connor Award for Short Fiction and was published by the University of Georgia Press (1985). This same work also received the Boston Globe Award and the Bay Area Book Reviewers Award for Fiction. She has won numerous other writing awards, including a PEN Syndicated Fiction Award and a National Endowment for the Arts (NEA) Award.

Ms. Giles's fiction has been widely published in journals and magazines, including *Redbook, San Francisco Review of Books Literary Supplement, New England Review*, and *Five Fingers Review*.

She won the National book Critics Circle Citation for Excellence in Book Reviewing in 1991. Her book reviews have appeared in the *Washington Post*, the *New York Times*, the *Los Angeles Times*, and the *San Jose Mercury News*.

She has a masters degree in English and is an associate professor at San Francisco State University. Acknowledged by her well-known students for her keen eye and ear for a story and for her writing abilities, Giles has also taught such bestselling novelists as Amy Tan and Gus Lee in writing workshops. She lives in Woodacre, California.